Dream Daddy

DALY THOMPSON

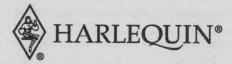

TORONTO • NEW YORK • LONDON
AMSTERDAM • PARIS • SYDNEY • HAMBURG
STOCKHOLM • ATHENS • TOKYO • MILAN • MADRID
PRAGUE • WARSAW • BUDAPEST • AUCKLAND

Recycling programs
for this product may
not exist in your area.

ISBN-13: 978-0-373-75312-3

DREAM DADDY

Copyright © 2010 by Barbara Daly / Mary E. Lounsbury.

This edition published by arrangement with Harlequin Books S.A.

For questions and comments about the quality of this book please contact us at Customer_eCare@Harlequin.ca

® and TM are trademarks of the publisher. Trademarks indicated with ® are registered in the United States Patent and Trademark Office, the Canadian Trade Marks Office and in other countries.

www.eHarlequin.com

Printed in U.S.A.

"You can persuade them. You're very good at that."

Ian didn't say the words. He didn't have to say them. They both knew what he was thinking, and it had been nice of him not to come right out and say, "You can con them, just the way you conned me."

But Tansy refused to feel bad about how she'd *persuaded* him to participate in the festival. It was good for him. Already he was opening up and having real conversations.

"You're right. I guess I am good at persuading people. Maybe I can find someone I can persuade to help."

"Trust me. They won't stand a chance," he said, and gave her a quirk of a smile.

The smile was so unexpected and enticing that Tansy found herself laughing. Ian looking happy was something she could get used to really fast.

Dear Reader,

Do opposites really attract? Ian Foster is reserved, grumpy, as introverted a man as ever existed. He's comfortable and satisfied with his predictable life. After a chaotic childhood, he welcomes stability. Sure, his life may be a little dull, but what's wrong with that? Dull is good. Dull is dependable.

The last woman in the world he wants to be with is Tansy Appletree, an exuberant redhead, mayor of the town of Holman and an enthusiastic extrovert. She's also the only CPA in Serenity Valley, and when Ian needs her professional services, she turns his life upside down.

Soon he's agreeing to all sorts of things, like helping with the town's upcoming festival. Because of Tansy, his quiet, organized world is soon a thing of the past. At first, the whirl of activity that surrounds Tansy drives him crazy, but all too soon, he starts to welcome a little excitement in his life. After all, too much predictability can be boring, and what could be more exhilarating than falling in love?

We hope you enjoy reading *Dream Daddy* as much as we enjoyed writing it, and we hope you find a little excitement in your own life—just like Ian.

Happy reading!

Barbara and Liz

ABOUT THE AUTHOR

Daly Thompson is a collaboration between Liz Jarrett and Barbara Daly, both accomplished writers. Liz has been writing stories since she was a child. After graduating from college, she was a technical writer for twelve years before she decided to stay home with her children. During their naps, she started writing again, this time focusing on fiction. She naturally turned her attention to her favorite type of stories— romances.

From early childhood, Barbara Daly has been a reading addict. She hid books under her mattress to read well past her bedtime, learned to cover a novel with her geography book and spent her allowance on Nancy Drew mysteries instead of school lunches. There is no twelve-step plan for this particular addiction. After a series of jobs that didn't come with built-in reading time, she settled on writing romance, which allows her the best of both worlds.

Books by Daly Thompson

HARLEQUIN AMERICAN ROMANCE
1272—ONE OF A KIND DAD
1297—SURPRISE DAD

Chapter One

Ian Foster came in from the barn, went automatically to his office, sat down at his desk and began to go through the mail.

A promotional offer for direct TV. Imbeciles—didn't they know he already had it? He tossed the flyer into the wastepaper basket. Next was a bill. He frowned, then put it in the "bills" folder and picked up the last envelope.

It was addressed to Foster Brothers, Inc., and the return address was Internal Revenue Service. He opened it with interest. Maybe the corporation he and his brothers had formed was getting a tax refund. They couldn't possibly owe more money—Ian had calculated the numbers too carefully, checking and double-checking.

He read it, and frustration rose from the pit of his stomach and emerged as a shout loud enough to rattle the paper clips on his desk. Man, why now? This was the last thing they needed. He slumped in his chair, put his head on his desk and held his breath.

"You dead? If you are, nod so I can start CPR."

Ian leaped up from his desk to confront his brother Daniel. "Of course I'm not dead."

"Do you feel faint?"

"Do I look like I feel faint? What the hell's wrong with you?"

Daniel's expression informed Ian that Daniel was thinking. Maddening trait of Daniel's—thinking before he spoke. "I'm on the way back from the barn where I've been inspecting your sheep," he said in that reasonable tone that drove Ian crazy, "and I hear a cry of pain from my brother, so I run into the house, find him collapsed at his desk, so I assume heart attack, and my first thought is to save his life. It's a natural reaction, Ian." His bedside manner also drove Ian crazy.

"For a cardiologist, maybe."

"Okay," Daniel said, "so what happened?"

Ian simply handed over the letter.

Daniel's smile faded. "Ah, the corporation's being audited. So what? You haven't lied or cheated or..."

Ian glared at him. "Of course not." He motioned his brother toward a leather-covered armchair. Why he bothered, he didn't know. Daniel knew he could sit down. "Auditors probe," he said. "Maybe they'll probe into why we formed the corporation, into who we are. If they find out who we are, and I'm sure the IRS has CIA-type information systems, then we're done for."

"Why would the IRS care about our past as long as we're paying our taxes?"

"Not the IRS, Serenity Valley," Ian moaned.

"You think the IRS would tell the neighbors?"

"You never know," Ian said, narrowing his eyes. "The auditor might be a local. He tells his wife, she tells her sister, who tells the preacher's wife, who tells the preacher... You know what it's like around here."

"Whoa," Daniel said. "You're thinking way too far ahead."

"I like being ready for the worst."

"Still," Daniel said, "if there's nothing wrong with the return and the documentation is in order, nothing will attract their attention. You have everything on disk, right? The books? The return?"

Ian cleared his throat. "The return itself looks professional."

"What are you telling me?"

"Well..." He had to confess. "I never quite got the hang of that accounting software." He pulled a clothbound volume out of his side drawer. "Here are our books." Then he produced his spreadsheet. Handwritten.

Daniel paled. "Geez, Ian. Where's your abacus?"

Feeling hurt, Ian displayed a handheld calculator.

"How did you get through business school?"

"I don't know. By being charming?"

"No," Daniel said, sounding resigned, "by coming up with the right answers in your own primitive way. But hey, it doesn't matter. You're overreacting. If there's nothing wrong with our numbers, why would they—"

"What if some little thing is wrong? If they get interested in us..."

Ian's worry wasn't financial, but personal. Of course the Foster Corporation, Inc. return was accurate—it would have been accurate down to the last penny if the government didn't insist on rounding off the numbers. He had a much more important reason to want to panic, and Daniel knew perfectly well what it was.

Putting it bluntly—he didn't know how to put things any other way—the Fosters weren't Fosters, or even brothers. They'd met in a juvenile correction facility, had bonded because of their mutual goal—to leave their pasts behind and get ahead in the world by working hard. And most of all by supporting one another, understanding that they each had a separate, very different career goal, and sacrificing whatever it took to make sure that each of them reached that goal.

They'd done it. Managed to get Daniel through veterinary school, and now he was Serenity Valley's most respected vet—its only vet, actually, but highly thought of. Sent Mike to culinary school, and now Mike's Diner was raking in the money—and the rave reviews for Mike's culinary skills. Respect was what it took to make it in this closed-in valley where everybody knew everybody else and newcomers were subjected to intense scrutiny.

Ian's degree was in animal husbandry, and after deciding that Daniel and Mike were hopeless with money, he got a second degree in business and took on the responsibility for their financial security. Now he could ruin them. It was a lot to think about.

Daniel gazed at him thoughtfully. "You might want to turn this audit over to someone else," he said.

"You think I can't handle it?" Ian's pride was involved here. As the youngest of the brothers, he had to prove that he could take care of them as well as they'd taken care of him. They'd put him in charge of the family financial affairs. If they ever decided they couldn't trust him, he'd have to opt out of the family, change his name and start all over.

Yes, he needed to be prepared for the worst-case scenario, because he'd lived through a few of them already. He tuned in to what Daniel was saying.

"You can't handle it tactfully," Daniel said, less than tactfully. "For example, 'none of your business' might not be the best thing to say to the auditor."

Daniel was right. That was exactly what Ian would have said if the auditor had cornered him. Neither tact nor subtlety was in his skill set. "Who should I turn it over to?" he said.

Daniel thought for a moment. "Tansy Appletree's the only tax accountant in the valley," he said. "Hire her."

"No way," Ian growled.

"Why not?"

Because she's too short to have any brains, and besides, she's way too energetic. "Well, because…" Daniel was waiting, with that irritatingly patient look on his face.

"Because she's also the mayor of Holman, her father is our state senator, her brother is planning to run for governor, so I don't trust her, either," Ian blurted out. "If she suspected anything, she'd spill it. And she'll be looking for things, too." He got up and began to pace. "Everybody in the valley is curious about us, especially about me, because I haven't gotten 'involved,' as they like to say, in the community."

"So *get* involved, Ian."

Ian didn't want to be involved with anybody but Daniel and Mike and their ever-expanding families. "That's not what we're talking about."

"In a way it is. You're saying you don't trust them. Tansy's a great person, and she's been an excellent mayor. She and Lilah and Allie are friends, and besides, unlike others I could mention—" the look Daniel gave him was so intense, Ian felt pinned down "—she uses the most up-to-date software. In fact, Lilah and Allie call her their 'redheaded geek.' So why not give her a chance?"

Lilah was Daniel's wife. Mike and Allie had set a wedding date. Ian had learned to trust the women because his brothers clearly did, but it hadn't been easy.

Still, he'd make a better impression if he presented the auditor with professional-looking records to back up the return, so he guessed he should listen up. He ground his teeth. "I'll think about it."

"How long do you have to think?"

Ian glanced at the letter. "Not very long."

Daniel got up. "Now that we've solved that," he said cheerfully, "I'll get back to your sheep."

And about time, Ian thought. Unless Daniel irritated the sheep. If he did, their fleece would lose both quality and quantity, and— He gave up that worst-case scenario. He was clearly going over the edge.

ACCOMPANIED BY HER administrative assistant, the town clerk, and the three Holman selectmen—select-*persons*—Mayor Tansy Appletree stood in front of Holman's historic Town Hall and launched into her pitch. "We've finished the main room, we have electricity and plumbing—and we're out of money. We've bled the pockets of Holman down to the last penny. But I have an idea that would raise at least enough to paint the outside."

"A government grant?" one of the selectpersons said hopefully.

"We have one in the works, but it will be months before it comes through. And we *need* to paint. No, I'm thinking of a Winter Holiday Festival. Doesn't that sound like a lot of fun?"

She was greeted with blank stares. "Here's how I see it," she said, trying not to sound as enthusiastic as she had before, since she'd apparently scared them. "Come inside with me."

They trailed silently after her, through the tall, creaky front doors and into the main room of the Hall. Once upon a time, it had echoed with the sounds of music and dancing as well as the monotonous drone of town meetings. The mayor and the town clerk had had their offices here. They held out when the telephone service came to Holman—what did they need with a telephone when people could just walk in?—but when electricity came in the 1940s, they moved into a room in the public library, the first building to be wired. Since then, the hall had fallen into a state of disrepair. Even when it was put on the National Register of Historic Places, former city officials had looked the other way, horrified at the expense of restoring it to its former glory. But not Tansy. Town Hall had been her first priority when she'd been elected mayor. It was coming along, but not fast enough.

She waved her arms around to encompass the huge space. "Look how big it is," she said. "We could invite the best-known craftspeople in Vermont—not just Serenity Valley—to set up their booths…" She paused to make outlines of imaginary booths. "No charge, but we'd ask for ten percent of their gross sales to go to Town Hall."

That got a murmur out of them. She'd call it progress. "We'll decorate for the holidays. A huge tree, garlands, candles. The room will be festive, and if we hang enough wreaths and lights outside, that will hide the fact that it looks horrid and will continue to look horrid—" she fixed a stern gaze on them "—until we *paint*."

They still seemed dubious, which Tansy took to mean they were thinking it over.

"We could sell food, too," her assistant, Amy Winfree, said shyly. "Mulled cider would be good and it would make the room smell lovely."

"What a wonderful idea," Tansy congratulated her. "Cider, wedges of apple pie, ginger cookies—gingerbread! All at reasonable prices, of course. Maybe some of you know someone who'd like to donate the cookies…"

One of the three selectpersons was a female, Martha Latham. She stared daggers at her male colleagues until they cleared their throats, coughed or scraped their boots on the ground, and at last, one of them said, "Aggie's gingerbread is sort of famous around here. I imagine she'd make a couple of pans."

Martha breathed out an exasperated sigh and pinned him down with one of her accusatory "chauvinist pig" glares.

"I'd help her, of course," the man said hastily. "Turn on the oven, add something to something else."

"Ay-uh," the other one of them spoke up. "Polly would get a kick out of contributing some apple pies." He looked down his nose at both Aggie's husband and Martha. "And I can't help, because Polly won't let anybody into her kitchen."

"Thank you all," Tansy said earnestly, hoping to avoid an argument among the selectmen—or "persons," she reminded herself. "Now, besides food, we have to have top-notch people exhibiting and hopefully selling their work."

To her surprise, her captive audience warmed to this idea, coming up with crafts and the names of the craftspeople—including woodworkers, knitters, crocheters, quilters, a group of rug-hookers who delighted in calling themselves The Hookers, and makers of holiday tree ornaments. Tansy was writing as fast as she could on a legal pad she'd kept clutched under her arm in case the selectpersons segued from shock and rejection to cooperation.

She'd gotten them on her side. That's what a politician was, right? A persuader. But she'd made a vow to persuade only toward the best results for all concerned, the same vow her father had made, the same vow she knew her brother had made when he threw his hat into the ring of candidates for the governor of Vermont.

The Winter Holiday Festival would be good for the valley. It would bring the careers of the many Vermont crafters into the limelight. She paused in her reflection to think about press coverage in the newspapers.

It was a good project. An honorable project. And she'd see it through to its satisfying conclusion: Town Hall, freshly painted.

IAN WAS OUTSIDE WITH HIS sheep, feeling gloomy. The sheep were fine—high-quality merinos, the first breed the British settlers brought to Vermont, carefully chosen, carefully bred, religiously taken care of by Daniel—they didn't have a worry in the world. If only *he* had it as good as his sheep.

He petted a hogget, a half-grown lamb, to make himself feel better. Last thing in the world he wanted to do was hand this audit over to a woman. Okay, so he sounded sexist, but he wasn't. He just didn't trust women, not really, and he felt that way for good reason. They were undependable. At least some of the ones he had known had been. What if he turned his books over to Tansy Appletree, and she found something she could hold over him in those carefully penned numbers? What if she just left town right in the middle of shaping up his books?

The hogget, who'd ducked her head under Ian's hand to help him pet her in just the right places, said, "Baaa."

"Baaa, humbug?" he asked her. "I'm stupid to mistrust Tansy Appletree? You women. You all stick together." He looked down at her. "Come on, little girl, time to go inside and play with your cousins."

With a few deep breaths and some mental chest-pounding, he pulled himself together. He had to do it. The audit would be over and done with by the time he figured out how to load the software, after he'd figured out which software he needed, which he'd have to do before he loaded it and figured out how to use it—it made him tired just thinking about it.

In his office, Ian stared at the phone awhile, then noticed the time was getting close to five o'clock. He made himself look up the number in the slim phone book the Churchill Consolidated High School published and sold to raise funds, the book with only valley numbers, so no weeding through the names of outsiders. Clutching the book, he dialed.

"Mayor Appletree's office," a voice said.

Ian actually preferred speaking to an office instead of to a person. "This is Ian Foster," he said gruffly. "I'd like to make an appointment with Ms. Appletree. Tomorrow if possible." *Do it, get it over with, maybe she'll say no, I'd be off the hook, well, off that hook.*

"Mr. Foster." The woman on the other end sounded nervous. "Um, let me check her schedule. What would the appointment be in regard to?"

Remembering his conversation with Daniel, Ian stifled the "none of your business" retort that was on the tip of his tongue. "I'll tell her when I see her," he said instead, congratulating himself on being more tactful than Daniel could ever imagine he could be.

"Just a minute, then," she said timidly, and apparently consulted a calendar. "I see she's free tomorrow afternoon between three and four."

"Tomorrow at three," Ian said and hung up the phone.

"TOMORROW?" TANSY FROWNED at her assistant, Amy Winfree, who looked thoroughly cowed. "What do you think he wants?"

"He said he'd tell you when he saw you, and I was too scared to pressure him," Amy confessed. "You know, ask him the questions I'm supposed to, 'town, business or personal.'"

"I'm familiar with Ian Foster's manner of speaking, and anyone would be scared to push him," Tansy said to comfort her. "So we'll see what he wants tomorrow at three. Don't worry, Amy, I can handle him. Time for you to go home," she said, checking the big wall clock. "I'll see you—and Ian Foster—tomorrow. If he brings a lamb with him, you can babysit."

"Whatever helps," Amy said, still sounding desperate.

THE LIST OF THINGS IAN FOSTER could be lobbying for boggled Tansy's mind. The river between Holman and Churchill—was there a sewage problem? An invasion of powerboats?

His farm was five miles from the freeway. Even though most of the drivers who used the exit turned north to LaRocque to go to Mike's Diner, or across the river to the gas station in Churchill, was he here to complain about strangers in town?

Ian Foster was the oddest man she'd ever met—not that she'd had a one-on-one conversation with him. He owned a substantial acreage, a quarter of Holman's square miles, he raised sheep, he had two delightful brothers she knew well. She knew Daniel's wife, Lilah, and Mike's fiancée, Allie, even better. But at the family dinners she'd been invited to and Ian had shown up for, he'd never spoken to her. He'd always directed his attention toward his brothers and Daniel's boys, who for reasons she couldn't imagine, seemed to be crazy about him. A soft spot—another oddity for a man so tightly wrapped into himself.

It occurred to her that she'd been thinking negatively, imagining Ian was coming to make trouble. Why not try putting a positive spin on things?

Town: he'd like to contribute some of his land to a

worthy cause—a baseball field, a wildlife park, whatever might bring business to Holman, which was desperately in need of outside money. Its "hiding place" reputation had gone too far. Holman needed interlopers with cash in their pockets and something to spend it on.

Business: that one stumped her. Ian Foster was a businessman himself. What could he possibly want from her in that area?

Personal: he wanted to ask her to go out with him.

Her heart did a little quickstep. He was grumpy, almost a recluse—and yet, somehow, the most appealing man she'd encountered in her lifetime in Serenity Valley. He wasn't quite as tall as his brothers, but he had a presence that made him look like Paul Bunyan. His dark hair, dark eyes and dark outlook on life touched her in a way she didn't understand. Something was going on inside him, and she longed to know what it was.

Enough second-guessing. She'd know tomorrow what he wanted from her, and she could hardly wait.

Chapter Two

"Yes," Ian snapped, slamming the latest copy of *Sheep Talk* magazine down on his desk. He'd come to his office to calm down, but now that Daniel had called to check up on him, he was upset all over again. "I have an appointment with her at three."

"You sound like it's an appointment with a funeral director," Daniel remarked.

"Close to it," Ian said, dread creeping through him.

"I'm confident that as soon as you talk to her, you'll feel reassured that she can do the computer stuff. And I'm sure she can handle the auditor." Daniel was being reasonable, something Ian didn't need at the moment.

"She's a politician," Ian reminded his brother. "Knows how to suck up to people."

"I'd put it differently—like, she has good social skills."

And I don't. I mean, I really don't. I don't need social skills, because I don't want to be social. "I'll call you after it's over," Ian said. "Don't bug me until then."

Ian was in his truck, on his way to the appointment, when his cell phone rang. "Ian," his brother Mike said, annoyingly cheerful, as always, "I hear you have an appointment with Tansy. When?"

"Three."

"It's two-forty," Mike said.

"I know what time it is! I'm on my way."

"Good. I just wanted to be sure you didn't forget."

Ian clicked the end button forcefully. How *could* he forget? He'd hardly slept last night for the nightmares he'd had about it.

As he approached the village, he took several deep breaths, rehearsed his opening speech, which would impress Tansy with its forthrightness, straightened his shoulders, then pulled into a parking space.

TANSY FRANTICALLY SCANNED her office. Her desk was neat, for the first time in—well, maybe for the first time. Ian looked like an obsessive-compulsive type. She didn't want to take any chances. A pot of freshly made coffee stood at the ready on the credenza in her office, and in front of it, a plate filled with brownies and cinnamon sugar cookies.

She'd made the cookies herself, a secret she hoped wouldn't get out.

And last, she took a look at herself in the antique mirror above the credenza. Yikes! She slashed lipstick onto her mouth, powdered her nose and tried her best to get her hair into some sort of order that wouldn't make her look like Little Orphan Annie.

She tugged down her rust-colored pencil skirt, straightened her matching turtleneck...

Okay, enough. She was taking this too far. It was one

minute until three. She sat behind her desk and waited. For forty-two seconds.

"Mayor Appletree," Amy said formally as she opened the door, "Ian Foster to see you."

Tansy stood up. What a change! Amy usually shouted something like, "He's here."

And he *was* here—in a brown leather bomber jacket, tan corduroy trousers, a plaid shirt, brown work boots—and a ferocious scowl. "Hello, Ian—"

"I'm being audited." He sat down without being asked.

She blinked. She'd never be the politician her father was if she blinked like that when she was surprised. "I'm sorry to hear that. What a pain."

Into the silence, she said, "May I get you some coffee?"

"No."

"A brownie?"

"No."

"Then how can I help you?" Giving up on small talk, Tansy sat, folded her hands on her desk and gave him her full attention, just the way her father did when he was talking to a constituent. It usually got her the other person's full attention, but Ian wasn't a normal person. Handsome, though, if you could overlook the somewhat troll-like personality. Which she could.

"With the audit, of course."

"Of course," she murmured. "Although you're well known for your financial skills, and I can't help wondering what I can—"

"You can put it on a computer."

"Oh." She would *not* blink. But who in the twenty-first century didn't know how to use a computer to do his taxes?

"And represent me during the audit."

Now that made more sense. Al Capone could have represented himself better than Ian could. "I'd be happy to help you," Tansy said, smoothly, she hoped. "Where should we start?"

"I thought *you'd* know where to start," he said.

Politicians didn't sigh when they were exasperated, either. They smiled. "I do, actually. I'll need to look at your return and your documentation."

In answer, Ian handed her a paper-clipped document and two books. She glanced at the document—his tax return, looking like any other tax return.

"This is for a business," she said, feeling puzzled. "Oh, I see, you and your brothers formed a corporation."

She wondered why. Ian had his sheep farm, Daniel was a vet and Mike had a restaurant. To an auditor, that could look suspicious, as if they were trying to pass off personal expenses as corporate ones.

Ian was silently staring at her, so she smoothed out her frown and picked up one of the clothbound volumes. "Now, what are these?"

"My books."

That was easy enough to see, but— Tansy opened one book, and then the other. They actually *were* his books, neat columns of figures totaled at the bottom and on the right-hand side. Handwritten. "And the documentation for these numbers?" She looked at Ian expectantly.

He shifted in his seat. "Those are at home," he said.

"All right. Bring them in and I'll—"

For the first time, Ian looked uncomfortable rather than combative. "It won't be that easy," he said. "It's more like, um, a box of paper."

Tansy felt a little helpless. "You could bring in the box... No," she said, determined to help this man whether he wanted help or not. "I have a better idea. I'll come to your farm, organize the documentation, and while I'm there, I'll install all the right software on your computer—you do have a computer..."

"Of course I have a computer."

"...and show you how to use it, so next year you'll be all set to do it by yourself."

"I was doing it just fine myself until this came..." He waved a sheet of paper she assumed was his audit notification. "But even I know I can't hand the guy two books and a box of paper."

"Or gal," Tansy said absentmindedly, suddenly struck by the way his eyebrows winged up perfectly.

"What?"

She returned to the present. "The auditor could be male or female."

Ian blew out an impatient breath and gave her a "duh" look.

"You'll certainly make a better impression if your papers appear to be professionally done," she told him. "I'll come out to see you in the morning, if that's all right, and we'll go over what you have."

He stood up. "If that's the only way to do it. Call before you come." He picked up his tax return and his books, and started for the door.

"Wait," Tansy called out.

Ian halted and made a half turn toward her.

"I'm happy to do this for you," she said graciously, "in spite of my *very* heavy workload just now, but I want something from you in return." She'd been thinking about it this morning, and now, while she had him on the hook, was the time to land him.

WOULDN'T YOU KNOW IT? Here came the hard sell.

"I intend to pay you at your customary rates," Ian said flatly. It wasn't that he was desperate and easily taken.

"I know, but I want something else."

He waited, tensing. People like Tansy made him nervous. They liked to talk, to chat, get to know people.

He didn't. Talking made him nervous.

"You know we're restoring Town Hall…" she said, her voice bright and cheerful.

Oh, money. She wanted money. He turned back toward the door. "I gave already."

"And *very* generously." She looked up into his face, gazing at him with her green eyes. "We appreciate it so, so much."

How did she do that? A second ago she'd been sitting behind her desk, and now she was in front of him, blocking the door.

"But you know we still have so much more to do." Tansy sighed, then perked up. "I had this brilliant idea, and the town selectpersons have agreed with it. We're holding a Winter Holiday Festival in the Town Hall!"

What did she expect him to say, "Yay, I can't wait?"

"What we're going to do," she said, herding him toward the long table that stood against one wall and handing him the cup of coffee he'd refused earlier, "is invite Vermont craftsmen—"

"Craftspeople," Ian said. Ha! One point for him.

Tansy put a hand over her mouth. He guessed she thought it looked pretty cute. "Oh, my goodness, thank you. If you hadn't reminded me, I'd have been in trouble before I even got this project off the ground. Want a brownie?"

Apparently he didn't actually have a say in the matter. A brownie on a little white napkin sat in his other hand.

"Anyway," Tansy went on, "we'll invite these craftspeople to set up booths in the hall and sell their work, then donate a percentage of their gross sales to the Town Hall fund."

Ian sensed trouble ahead. Silence was his best bet.

"But we also want to have demonstrations of the various crafts, how they're made and so on. I was thinking this morning that it would be wonderful if you'd set up a 'sheep to sweater' booth."

What the hell was she talking about?

"I see the booth divided into three sections. In the first one, we'd show you, or one of your hands shearing a sheep. In the second, someone would be spinning the wool, and in the third, knitting a sweater. Doesn't that sound good?"

She was so excited about the stupidest idea he'd ever heard that her red hair was starting to spring out into little curls around her face.

"You don't shear sheep in the winter," he informed her. "You'd have to keep them in the house if you did."

"One sheep?" she said, looking at him hopefully.

"Shear a little of it each time someone comes by the booth? I know!" She clapped her hands. "I bet anything the school would like to keep a sheep somewhere for the winter."

"The school…" Was she insane? And where would he come up with spinners and knitters? His wool was spun and knitted by machines in huge textile mills down south. He said goodbye to his wool as soon as it was baled.

Tansy barreled on. In fact, she was starting to make him dizzy, or maybe it was a sugar rush from the brownie he seemed to have eaten. "I'm sure we can get someone to come down from one of the historical museums to spin the yarn, and, of course, the valley is full of expert knitters. Have another brownie, or maybe you'd like a cookie."

"No, th—" And there was the cookie on another little napkin.

"Just think it over." She got a look on her face Ian really didn't like. "Think how much the kids would enjoy it."

She was pushing his buttons. He had to leave before she pushed harder—but he was already too late.

"Speaking of kids," she continued, "I am so proud of what Daniel accomplished by getting the Foster Care Center on its way. It will give those children a wonderful home to replace the one they've been taken out of."

"Yeah," he muttered around a mouthful of cookie crumbs. On a wedge of his land a complex was rising up out of the pasture, a facility designed to house foster children in individual homes each with a live-in couple to act as mother and father to a family of six. It was

Daniel's idea and second in his heart only to his wife and his own foster kids.

"It was hard to convince the valley people, but he did it. I tried to help him all I could," she said earnestly. "With those permits he needed and leaning on the other two mayors. Gosh, were they ever stubborn."

So that was what this was about. She'd help him with his taxes and help Daniel with the many remaining details of the foster care center if he'd shear a sheep for openmouthed kids.

"I'll think it over and tell you tomorrow," he said as he snagged another brownie, serpentined past her and at last made it out the door.

Mayor Appletree was little, but she was tough.

TANSY COLLAPSED AGAINST the credenza, staring after Ian. Then she stared for a while at the almost-full pot of coffee, the brownies and cookies she'd labored over the night before. Feeling spacey, she went into the outer office where Amy sat.

"Nice chat?" Amy asked brightly.

"You wouldn't believe me if I told you." She paused. "I had to play my ace, and now I feel guilty."

"You have to do what you have to do," Amy said primly. "I think he'll agree."

Tansy's mouth dropped open. "Were you eavesdropping?"

"On the intercom," Amy said without a touch of remorse. "You handled it well, like a true politician."

"Don't release a word of this to the valley gossip chain," Tansy warned her.

"No need. Three people already called to see what your business was with Ian Foster."

Tansy sighed. "Well, don't tell them. You know, I need a lift. How about joining me for a cup of coffee and about six brownies?"

ON THE WAY BACK TO THE FARM, Ian fumed. The nerve of that woman, blackmailing him like that. It wasn't as though he wasn't paying her for getting him ready for the audit.

Her brownies were awesome. He wondered when she planned to run for president. After being lobbied by her, he thought she had a decent chance at it.

The cookies weren't bad, either. Maybe he could have Amos shear a sheep and a yearling, let the kids see the difference in the wool, explain why lambswool is more expensive than sheep's wool.

The barn was heated, but perhaps not enough. He guessed the two shorn sheep could stay in the finished part of the basement for the winter.

He realized he'd stopped being mad at Tansy. This was a bad sign. So when Lilah called to ask him for a very impromptu dinner—that's what she called it—he didn't argue as much as usual. Being with his family—his huge, extended family—might shake some sense into him.

But when he arrived, looking forward to such loud babble going on all around him that he wouldn't need to say much, the first person he saw was Tansy. He almost turned and ran.

But where would he go? They'd seen him, and he wasn't that rude. Not quite.

So he just directed his attention elsewhere. Except for Tansy's presence, the party was going the way all Daniel's family parties went—loudly and actively. Daniel, three of his foster boys and Lilah's son were bundled up against the November cold and deep into a soccer game in the endless backyard behind Daniel's Queen Anne Victorian house. Tansy, in a neon orange jacket, was on the sidelines, yelling like a one-woman pep squad. He could see Jesse, Daniel's friend and general factotum, through the kitchen window, stirring and bending down to look into the oven at the same time. Lilah and Allie, pink-faced and swathed in parkas, were leaping up from the summery lawn chairs and making a beeline for him.

"Ian!" Lilah said, giving him a big hug. "I'm so glad you came. We invited Tansy, too, and luckily she was free."

"Say hi to Uncle Ian," Allie said to the globe of red snowsuit in her arms, apparently Brian, the baby Mike had literally inherited.

"Eeeeeeeeee," Brian screeched from the depths of his hood.

"Hi, big guy," Ian said. He smiled at the kid—hard not to—but didn't hold out his arms for him. He didn't know what to do with a baby and figured it was best to leave him in dependable hands.

"Mike will drop by for a minute," Allie told him. "He's training some new people and you can hardly pry him out of the restaurant."

Ian thought of something pleasant he could say. "How's the new house?"

"New *old* house," Allie corrected him. "Something

falls apart every day, but we love it. Tansy!" she called out, and to his dismay, Ian saw his new accountant spin away from the game and toward him, very possibly planning to speak to him.

"Gotta play soccer," he mumbled, and threw himself into the game.

But he wasn't safe yet. Tansy sat beside him at the big round table in Daniel's kitchen. On a happy note, Daniel's foster child Nick, as redheaded as Tansy, sat on his other side. Ha! Somebody trustworthy to talk to.

"That was a great save you did out there as goalie," he told Nick.

The boy beamed. "And you kicked it."

"Hard as I could," Ian lied.

Of all the boys that had flowed through Daniel's house, this boy was the only one Ian had ever, well, what would you call it, felt a little bit close to? Nick's past was a mystery. He'd just showed up one day with no name and no history anyone could coax out of him.

Ian had thought his own past had toughened him up enough that nothing could ever touch his heart—until he got to know Nick. At least Ian knew exactly why *he'd* ended up on the street, been arrested for shoplifting, and had been sent to the juvenile correctional facility. His mother had constantly been in an alcoholic stupor, and one day, she'd left and hadn't come back. Ian took care of himself by mowing lawns and sleeping in the park, stealing and sneaking into a church to sleep in winter, living out of a backpack, until the police picked him up. He remembered everything, and even now, when his life had straightened out, he couldn't escape the nightmares.

Maybe it was better not knowing, and Nick had decided not to remember. Or maybe just not to tell what he remembered.

"How are you, Nick?" Tansy leaned around Ian to give Nick a warm smile. Her hair tickled his chin, and it smelled of coconut and lime. Ian drew back, which only gave her room to get closer to him.

"I'm fine," Nick said shyly. "I'm making good grades."

"Do you like your classes?"

"Most of them, but especially art."

Startled, Ian jumped. "Aha, an artist in the family," Tansy said, and she didn't say it teasingly. She said it as if being an artist were the finest thing one could do with one's life. "What kind of art do you like to do? Painting? Sculpture?"

"I don't know yet." Nick ducked his head.

"You don't need to," she told him. "You have years and years to try new things."

"Speaking of which," Lilah said, "are you still serious about running for state office?"

Tansy sighed. "Oh, yes. I guess it's in my blood. I have a long way to go, though. First, I want to be a good mayor. Then we'll see."

"I heard you're planning a big holiday crafts market," Allie said.

"*Where* did you hear it?" Tansy asked.

"Well, you were standing out in front of Town Hall with all the town officials, and Hannah Hopewell was just too curious not to sneak up on you and listen, but I didn't hear it from Hannah, I heard it from—"

Tansy held up a hand. "Don't even tell me. Everybody

knows now, and I guess that's good. I bet I'll get dozens of suggestions for booths and exhibits. Incidentally…"

Don't say it, don't say it…

"I've asked Ian to set up an exhibit showing how fleece turns into yarn and yarn into—"

Daniel stared at him. "Ian, that's fabulous," Lilah said.

"That'll be fun," another of the boys said. "Will you shear a real sheep?"

"Well, I—"

"Of course he will," Tansy enthused. "And a lamb. They're so cute. Do you, ah, ever sell any of them for—"

"My lambs are not food," Ian snapped.

"He's religious about it," Allie said. "He made Daniel promise not to feed the kids lamb, and Mike never serves it in the restaurant."

"But you're not a vegetarian," Tansy said. "You're putting away the roast pork like you haven't eaten in three days."

"Just lamb," Ian growled. "Lambs aren't for eating."

"Oh," Tansy said softly, "you must really love them."

"I make money off the wool," Ian said, not giving an inch. "You get a rack of lamb, or you get the wool. I'm after the wool."

There was a brief, uncomfortable silence, and Ian wished he hadn't sounded so materialistic. But in seconds the noise level rose and everything seemed to be back to normal, except for the thoughtful way Tansy glanced at him now and again.

So he felt sort of protective about his sheep. What was so weird about that?

Mike blew in at eight, smelling like basil, and in his annoying way, instantly woke everybody up from their postdinner drowsiness and made them laugh.

Except him. He loved his brothers—they were the only humans in the world he trusted—but he worried about them. They gave out too much of themselves. Why couldn't they understand how dangerous that was, how badly they could get hurt with so many chinks in their armor? He'd kept his in perfect condition for years, thank you very much, and didn't intend to change.

"This was great. Gotta go," he said as soon as he thought he could without offending his family.

Out of the chorus of goodbyes, all he remembered were Nick's "Bye, Uncle Ian," and Tansy's "I'll see you tomorrow at nine," and both of them looking as if they wished he'd stay.

IN THE KITCHEN, HELPING with the cleanup, Tansy watched Mike wolf down the last of the brownies she'd brought to the party and said, "My brownies are pretty good, aren't they?"

"The best," Lilah said. "We opened the high school bake sale at nine, and they were gone by nine-fifteen."

"I had to force Ian to eat one," Tansy said.

Her face heated up, that telltale blush she'd gotten stuck with by being a redhead, when she saw the way everyone in the kitchen gazed at her. Were they thinking, "Ian came in for an appointment, and she made brownies for him? That's pathetic."

"That's just Ian," Daniel said.

"You'll get used to him," Lilah added. "Look at the way the boys love him, and he never even smiles at them."

From the doorway, Nick, his hands full of knives and forks, said, "Uncle Ian's nice. He just pretends he isn't."

Now their gazes were riveted on the little boy rather than on her. "That's it in a nutshell," Allie murmured.

He just pretends he isn't. Okay, if Ian Foster had some "nice" in him, Tansy intended to find it.

Chapter Three

Ian knew he'd always been a little bit obsessive-compulsive—a reaction to the chaos in his early life, a psychologist had told him—but even he knew that this time he was taking it a little too far. He'd been up since five to give himself time to shower and shave, to get his farm up and going for the day, and most important, to get ready for the onslaught of Tansy Appletree.

He was going over his office inch by inch, looking for anything personal that Tansy might glom on to. Not that he thought she'd snoop around for information about him, but what if something just fell out of a file drawer? She'd pick it up, and naturally, she'd read it….

He was losing his mind. Things didn't fall out of hanging folders in file drawers. However logical that was, it wasn't making the slightest impression on him.

He'd moved the files containing his criminal record, his release-from-prison papers and the documents showing that he, Daniel and Mike had legally changed their last names to Foster into his bedroom and slid them neatly between the mattress and box springs. But when he realized he was looking for a place to hide his grocery bills, he thought he'd better stop drinking coffee before he burned everything in the office except the tax stuff.

Tansy would be here at nine. A thought struck him—she'd had coffee and those great brownies ready for him yesterday afternoon. Maybe that's how you were supposed to do things. Maybe he should have a fresh pot of coffee and a coffee cake ready to serve her.

Good idea. And he knew how to make coffee cake. First, open the box of coffee cake mix....

WHILE TANSY DROVE THE FIVE miles to Ian's farm, she made a list of rules for herself. *Be calm and polite at all times. Don't let yourself get mad, even inside, no matter how gruff he is. Do the job right, even if he never says thank you.*

She glanced down at herself. Were her clothes okay? She'd decided to look professional, wear her toast-colored pantsuit with a cream silk blouse. Would he think she was trying too hard? Would jeans have been a better choice for a farmhouse call?

It was the first time she'd worried about a job since she passed her CPA exams.

The house sat at the end of a long driveway, set well back from the road. It was small and rustic-looking, with brown-stained clapboards, gray trim and a handsome slate roof. Old or new, she couldn't tell, but it looked as if it had been there forever.

When she pulled up beside it, she gave herself a moment to gaze at Ian's property—meadows and rolling hills in the near distance, white-dotted with sheep, forest at the foot of the slope and snowcapped mountains in the background. A sight like this should soothe anyone's soul. Maybe that's why Ian never went anywhere he didn't have to—he was happiest here.

He didn't look it when he answered the door. He nodded at her and said, "Come in."

He led her through a foyer. To the left she saw a living room that was surprisingly warm-looking with its rust-red walls, leather furniture and several antique pieces. To the right was a dining room painted the same color, and in the center of the room, under a simple pewter chandelier, was a round maple table almost identical to Daniel's.

She hid a smile. Ian must entertain his family, even if no one else, and the table had to be big enough for everybody.

But they'd reached his office, and although it was decorated much like the other two rooms she'd had a chance to peek into, the first thing she noticed was its neatness. Books stood perfectly straight in the bookshelves. Stacks of magazines were squared off. Not a shred of paper was in sight. The large antique desk that faced the doorway held a lamp, a printer, a fax machine, wooden desk accessories—and a huge, squat monitor.

Another clue—she had her work cut out for her if she was going to update his computer system.

But then her eyes widened. On a small table that sat beside the single armchair were a coffeepot and a coffee cake that gave off a delicious odor of cinnamon and toasted pecans.

"Coffee?" he mumbled.

"Absolutely," she said, "and if you don't offer me a piece of that coffee cake immediately, I'll have to steal some."

He handed her a cup of coffee first. Black, without asking her if she wanted cream and sugar, which was fine, because that was how she liked it. Black and strong.

While he cut the coffee cake—good grief, he actually had a ruler positioned over the baking dish while he cut—she took a sip. Wow. Talk about strong.

"This is fabulous," she enthused. "Just what I needed."

He turned away from his methodical cutting. "This is early for you?"

Tansy gathered that he disapproved of sleeping late. "Oh, no, I'm awake by seven at the latest."

The look he gave her indicated that seven *was* late. She should have said six, or even four. The truth was, she'd been up half the night, dreading this encounter, and had been dressed and ready to leave two hours early. And had spent thirty minutes of those two hours assessing herself in the mirror.

What was going on with her? He came toward her with a perfect square of coffee cake on a plate—a real plate, not paper—and she got a glimmer of what was going on with her.

Broad shoulders that carried his plaid shirt—almost certainly wool, given Ian's profession—perfectly, hinting at muscled arms. His jeans, not designer jeans as far as she could tell from her experience with mail-order catalogues, glided carelessly over a narrow waist, sloping hips and legs as muscular as she imagined his arms to be. The image ended at the same stout boots he'd worn for his appointment to see her.

That's what was going on with her, proximity to a

gorgeous man who didn't want to admit he was a nice man, too. Tansy longed for the first bite of him—oops, Freudian slip, she meant the first bite of his coffee cake.

"Fabulous" was the word that drifted out of her mouth, and just as she was about to start blushing, he said, "Here's the box of stuff—" he pulled it out of a storage closet "—and here are my return and books." He left quickly, not even taking a perfect three-by-three-inch square of the coffee cake with him.

Okay. She was on her own. She took a look at the CPU stationed to the right of the knee space in his desk and booted it up to see what edition she'd be working with. Her heart sank when she saw it wasn't the latest, not even the second latest. Matched the clunky monitor, for sure.

Updating the computer could come later. Her first priority had to be the box of documentation, so she began sorting the various invoices, receipts and Daniel's and Mike's reports of gross income versus profits. *Their* spreadsheets were computer generated. Ian's records consisted of hundreds of little pieces of paper—gross income from his sales of fleece, minus…everything else in that box, she guessed.

She listed the reasons this tax return had sent up a red flag to the IRS. They might wonder, as she had, why the brothers had formed a corporation. Individuals who did that were occasionally looking for tax breaks, since corporations were taxed less heavily. But a quick glance at Daniel's and Mike's spreadsheets didn't reveal any personal expenses they'd tried to slip in as corporate deductions.

Everyone in the valley knew the Fosters as good, generous, upstanding citizens. She couldn't imagine them cheating.

The auditor might focus in on Daniel's being Ian's vet of choice, but then, Daniel was the only vet in the valley, so that should be easy to explain. No mystery why they all ate at Mike's Diner. It was the only restaurant in the valley that served dinner. And, of course, who could argue that one of the three brothers attended to the financial affairs of the corporation.

While these thoughts went through her mind, Tansy sorted. And sorted. And sorted. Then ate another piece of coffee cake, drank another cup of coffee and sorted some more.

It was odd that everything else was military-neat except these little pieces of paper. Well, they were neat, yes, piled in a box made of a variety of woods beautifully arranged and mitred. Unfortunately, the box was sixteen inches high. You could pack a lot of paper into a sixteen-inch pile, and it was filled to the brim.

By noon, every surface in the office was covered with short stacks of documentation that she'd sorted into categories. Tansy had taken off her jacket and rolled up her shirtsleeves, thank goodness, because her hands were stained with ink, and she'd suffered a couple of paper cuts. And at this point, she was cross-eyed from looking at fine print.

She heard footsteps in the hall. Ian peered through the door, scanned the room, moaned and fled.

She stared after him. *That's why these papers haven't been sorted. He couldn't handle the mess.*

SHE'D WRECKED HIS OFFICE! Three hours, and she'd destroyed his sanctuary! Would she leave it that way overnight? He'd have to hide out in his bedroom until she'd picked it all up.

No, he could pick it up, square off the stacks, turn them into one stack with pieces of paper turned crosswise between them.

Ian stalked into the kitchen, where his housekeeper, Edna, was cooking his lunch. "I fixed lunch for Tansy, too," she told him.

His brow furrowed. "Take a tray to her in my office," he said. *Her* office now, apparently.

Edna turned off the burner and limped toward him so she could look him straight in the eyes. "No," she said. "Mind your manners, Ian Foster. She'll have lunch right here with you at the kitchen table. You can have a nice visit."

Ian glanced at the kitchen table and gritted his teeth. It was set for two, and she'd put flowers in the middle. The woman had no respect for him. But he had enormous respect for her cooking and housekeeping skills, and didn't intend to cross her. "So go ask her."

"You do it."

"No." He'd stand firm on this one. "If you ask her, she'll know you cooked enough for her."

Shaking her head, Edna moved down the hall, exaggerating her bad leg, Ian thought. A minute later, he heard

Tansy's bright, enthusiastic voice, and it was coming closer. He steeled himself.

Edna came in first, carrying the coffee cake and frowning at him. He had a right to cook in his own house, didn't he? And to buy a couple of cake mixes and canned stew in case of an emergency?

"This is so nice of you," Tansy bubbled. "I'd just developed a strong aversion to paper."

"What will you do with all that stuff when you've sorted them?" Ian asked her, feeling anxious.

"Look at this," Tansy said delightedly when Edna put a plate in front of her. She picked up her fork and knife, then turned her attention back to him. "First, I'll put each category in a folder." She took a big bite. "Then I'll— Edna, this is delicious!"

"Just a little chicken and dumplings with a nice salad is all." But Edna looked pleased. "Apple crisp for dessert." Her frown returned. "Ian, you'll have to serve it. Do you know where to find the ice cream?"

"The freezer would be my guess," Ian said.

Tansy giggled. Had he said something funny?

"Aren't you going to eat with us?" Tansy asked Edna.

"Oh, no. I have to feed the farmhands, and Joe and Tim. Joe's my husband and Ian's handyman, Tim's the foreman."

"I hope I'll get to meet them," Tansy said.

As soon as Edna had wheeled a cart loaded with food down a ramp that substituted for a back stoop, her bad leg having improved considerably in the past few minutes, Tansy went back to bugging him again.

"Will you give me a tour of the farm after lunch? My

eyes really are strained." She gave him an earnest, wide-eyed look he knew was supposed to make him say yes.

And it worked. "All right," he heard himself saying.

"I won't charge you for the time it takes for lunch and the tour," she said.

He waved a hand.

"I have to warn you, Ian, that it's going to take me several days to get your books in shape. And the computer's another matter altogether. But I know how to upgrade it. I'll do my best." She smiled at him.

Ian mumbled, "Yes, okay, sure," and dived into the chicken and dumplings. It was just a little after twelve, and he was flat-out used-up.

"IT'S SO BEAUTIFUL." TANSY sighed. So was the man walking beside her, walking fast, as if he could hardly wait to get the tour over with.

"Good grazing land" was all Ian said.

"Was your house already on the property when you bought it?"

"Mmm-hmm."

"You restored it?"

"And added a couple of things, like plumbing and electricity."

Encouraged by such a long sentence, Tansy turned her attention to the outbuildings. "The barn's gigantic," she breathed.

"I have a lot of sheep."

If he ever decided to write poetry, he shouldn't give up his day job.

The barn was at least five times as large as the house and painted the traditional rust-red. She was suddenly amused that he'd also painted so many rooms in his house barn-red. What could be more appropriate?

The southeast end of the barn looked a little different from the rest. Following the slope of the land, it was two stories in height, its second floor level with the original barn, and it had, of all things, skylights in the roof. "That's a new addition, isn't it?"

"Yep."

He rushed her past it, and she scurried along behind him.

"Whose house is that?" she asked, pointing to another structure.

"Bunkhouse."

It was actually a house. Bigger than Ian's, she thought. Wow, his farmhands slept in comfort.

"Oh, my goodness," she said, "more barns."

"Place used to belong to a dairy farmer."

That didn't mean anything to her, but apparently it was all she was going to get.

"Ian," a voice called out.

She turned to see a man striding toward them. "Joe," Ian said, and met him halfway. Tansy hurried to catch up. She assumed this was Edna's husband, and she wanted to meet him. When she drew close, she saw that instead of a left hand, he wore a prosthesis. What had happened, she wondered, to damage Edna's leg and Joe's hand?

"Got a little problem with the heating system I can't fix," Joe said.

"I'll take a look at it," Ian said. He cast a glance back at Tansy. "Um, Tansy Appletree, Joe."

"Ma'am," Joe said, and held out his good hand.

Graceful introduction, smooth, concise. "Explore all you want to," he told her, and went with Joe toward the barn. Another man, tall and fair-haired, jogged across the meadow, gesturing at Ian. To her amazement, Ian began answering the man with gestures of his own. Ian knew sign language?

Good manners—no, admit it, sheer curiosity—required Tansy to catch up with them, too. Ian scowled at her, but she ignored it. "And this is?" she asked him.

"Tim," Ian said, clipping off the word.

"Tell him who I am," she insisted.

Ian sighed, then began to sign rapidly. Tim smiled and held out his hand.

"Oh, you're the foreman," Tansy said.

Ian signed to Tim, then growled, "My farmhands are terrified of him, as you might imagine."

Well. Would wonders ever cease? Ian had shown compassion when he hired Joe, Edna and Tim, and now it seemed he even had a little bit of a sense of humor—a very little bit, but anything was better than nothing.

He signed what he'd said to Tim, who smiled even more broadly. "If we're through with the social part," he said to Tansy, glaring down at her, "I have a broken heating unit and a farmhand to fire. And you—" he pointed a finger at her "—have a job to do."

The three of them disappeared into the depths of the barn, deserting her.

She stared after them and decided it wouldn't be wise to follow them. And, as he'd said, she had a job to do.

Slowly she went into Ian's office and went back to sorting.

"MIGHTY NICE LADY, TANSY IS," Joe said.

"Mmmph," Ian muttered from the bowels of the furnace. Joe knew a heck of a lot more about furnaces than he did, and probably knew exactly what was wrong, but wouldn't dream of going out to buy parts without a thumbs-up from Ian. So his search through unidentifiable moving parts was part of their ritual.

"Been a good mayor, ay-uh," Joe said.

"She hasn't stolen anything as far as we know," Ian said.

"Edna said she's doing some work for you."

"Yep."

"Said she sure seemed to enjoy the chicken and dumplings."

Ian sighed. This was only the first day and he was already tired of having Tansy around. He'd welcomed the ailing furnace, thinking it would give him a nice break, and then Joe had to bring her up. It was time to change the subject. "Well, Joe, there sure is something wrong here," he said, wiping his hands on some rough brown paper towels. "Any idea what it might be?"

"I'm thinking it might need a new thermostat."

"That would be my guess, too. Can you get hold of one?"

"I'll have to drive to Rutland, I imagine," Joe said.

"Take Edna with you," Ian said. "Give her a little time out from the housekeeping."

"Thanks, boss," Joe said. "I'll go see if she's got dinner far enough along to let me drag her away."

Tim waited in the office he kept in the barn. Ian stepped in and signed, "What's up with Nathan?"

Tim signed rapidly.

"Drinking on the job?" Ian signed back, gesturing wildly in his anger. "He knows the rules!"

He took in Tim's response and said, "I know he's a

good worker, but I can't have anybody on my payroll who drinks on the job." If he had his way, nobody would drink anything anywhere, anytime, but he couldn't control other people's lives, just the part they spent taking care of his sheep.

Tim nodded and gestured toward his desk.

Ian sighed. "No, not yet," he signed. "I'd better talk to him first."

Tim smiled. Yeah, yeah, Ian hated to fire his people. But he wasn't an old softie, which Tim seemed to be suggesting he was. He'd give Nathan a tongue-lashing he'd never forget.

"Nathan," he said gently a few minutes later, "I can't have any of my hands drinking. You know that. You think you can give me your solemn promise not to do it again?"

TANSY COULDN'T SEE AN END to the sorting; she was still only a third of the way through the box. But she couldn't concentrate. She realized she was staring dreamily at each piece of paper, then drifting from one stack to the next, looking for the right category, when this morning, she'd known exactly which was which.

She had to shape up. She was racing along, back to her old speed, when she hit a snag. The snag was a bill for clothes, jeans, shirts and work boots. It was such a large bill, for so many clothes, that she guessed the clothes were for his farmhands. Either way, she'd better ask Ian while it was on her mind.

Hmm. *Be honest, Tansy. It's an excuse to see him for a minute or two.* Was she getting some kind of weird fixation on the man? Maybe because he was unattainable?

She'd never imagined herself to be the kind of woman who wanted that kind of man.

She slipped on her coat and, carrying the bill in a folder, she went in search of him. Since she couldn't see him anywhere on the meadow, she went into the barn, wandering thoughtfully through the enormous shelters for the sheep during the coldest weather, a large shearing room, equipment, storage for hay.

Just to her left was a small office—Tim's, she guessed—but it was empty. She opened another door and laughed. The straw-covered room was filled with half-grown lambs. "You're so cute!" she said, petting one of them. They milled around her, bleating softly, their soft fleeces brushing against her. She knelt down to hug them and to let them nuzzle her. When she remembered she was here for a purpose, she stood up, brushing her hands together. Handling paper had made them feel dry. Now they were soft and silky again from the lanolin in the lambswool.

Would Ian's hands be soft in spite of the hard work he did? If he caressed her, would it feel like—

What was she thinking? All alone in the barn Tansy felt herself blushing.

She renewed her search. She hadn't found the sky-light room yet, so she couldn't give up. Near the end of the hall she discovered a door sheltered in a niche. She might have gone past it if she hadn't been looking for it.

She knocked, then walked in. A landing led down a set of stairs to a large room below. It was the skylight room, aglow from the sun that shone through the glass. The landing and stairs were enclosed. She called out

Ian's name, and not getting an answer, hesitated. The possibility that this room led to others sent her down the stairs. She reached the bottom step, turned into the room and gasped.

An explosion of color hit her like a tangible force. Bold, brutal slashes of color, fierce in their intensity.

The room was a studio, and it was filled with paintings.

Chapter Four

Tansy gripped the newel post for support, stunned by her discovery. The paintings were landscapes, but instead of serene hills, sparkling lakes and tree-shaded woodland clearings, they depicted the raw and sometimes brutal side of nature. They were mesmerizing. She studied them for minutes, hours, she couldn't tell, drinking them in. You didn't need to be an expert to know they were good. You could tell by the way they made you feel—frightened, scared, but beyond that, stirred by their energy.

Tim might be the creator of these paintings, but she didn't think so. Ian had to have done them. Closed inside himself, it was with brush and canvas that he expressed his wild, angry feelings.

Angry at what? That was none of her business. Neither were these paintings, but—

They were too good to be locked up in this room. The public deserved to see them.

And she knew exactly which slice of the public should see them first. Impetuously, she raced out of the barn, shrieking Ian's name.

WHEN IAN SAW TANSY STREAKING across the meadow, he had a feeling she was trouble on rollerblades. Her hair stood out around her head, and he could see those green eyes of hers flashing even at this distance.

"Uh-oh," he signed to Tim.

"I have something really important to do in the office," Tim signed back, and fled.

Ian set his jaw and waited for the onslaught.

"Ian," Tansy said breathlessly as she chugged up to him, "I have to tell you—" She halted. "I mean *ask* you. Is this bill personal or business?" She brandished a folder at him.

Nobody, *nobody* could get that excited about a bill. Suspicion bloomed inside him. She was up to something.

He opened the folder. "Business," he said when he saw the bill. "Work clothes for the hands."

"How thoughtful of you," she bubbled. "I should've known. It's typical of you. Hiring Edna and Joe, hiring Tim and learning sign language—you're a very sensitive person."

She had to be joking. Ian just stared at her.

"Well, you are, whether you know it or not. Have you ever, um, thought of expressing that sensitivity in some way, like writing, or…"

She'd found the paintings. He narrowed his eyes. He wasn't going to make it easy for her. He wanted to hear her confess that she'd been snooping around the barn, had barged into his studio, opened a closed door, invaded his privacy. For all he knew, she'd been getting into files in his office without permission. So he hadn't been paranoid when he hid the important stuff this morning. What he really wanted to do was fire her, but there was that audit to worry about. So he said, "Why do you ask? It's not a question people usually ask me. For obvious reasons."

"I just wondered. Maybe you knit? That can be a very artistic skill. Or do needlepoint?"

Was the woman insane? "No," he snapped.

"Quilting? Rug-hooking?"

He gave her a look, and suddenly she caved. "Okay, okay, I found the paintings." And then she astounded him by getting all excited again. No abject apologies, no explanations, nothing but shining eyes and hair getting wilder by the minute.

"They're wonderful," she breathed. "So strong, so expressive. Ian," she said earnestly, "you have to show them to other people. They're too good to keep locked away. And I have this brilliant idea—"

"No." Furious with her, he said the one word and strode away. It had taken him only a split second to figure out what her brilliant idea was, and he was having no part of it. He couldn't believe it when she began trotting along beside him, stumbling occasionally in her meadow-challenged accountant shoes, but keeping up with him nonetheless.

"You could show them at the festival. Sell them. Start making a name for yourself—I mean, you've already made a name for yourself in business, but—"

"No." Where the heck were the hands? Why couldn't one of them start yelling, "Coyotes!" making it absolutely necessary for him to escape? "I'm busy. I have work to do. I've already said I'd do that ridiculous sheep-to-shoulders booth—"

"Sheep-to-sweater," Tansy corrected him, still not in the least abashed.

"Well, that's enough. Time for somebody else to contribute to your festival."

"It's not *my* festival," she said, "it's the town's festival, our chance to raise money to finish restoring Town Hall, our chance to attract visitors to Holman." She'd gotten more enthusiastic with each phrase.

"What I like about Holman, the reason I moved here," he said, dropping each word like a brick, "was that it *didn't* attract visitors, and nobody had ever heard of it." He realized his voice had gotten as loud as hers, but he didn't care. "So the answer, for the last time, is no!"

Now he felt he had a perfect right to walk away. Twenty-five paces and he couldn't keep himself from turning back. Tansy was moving toward the house, her shoulders slumped in discouragement. Ian suddenly felt bad. Damn it! He didn't have anything to feel bad about!

ALONE IN IAN'S OFFICE, Tansy scrutinized her inner being and decided she was a spoiled brat. She was too accustomed to getting her own way by persuading people that they wanted to do what she wanted them to do, that maybe they'd actually thought up the idea themselves.

She'd had no right to invade Ian's privacy and uncover his deep, dark secret, which was actually quite colorful. She shouldn't have tried to talk him into showing his paintings to the public. She was sorry she'd done it, because...

Because she should have approached him another

way. Tansy whistled softly while she continued sorting Ian's tax receipts. She hoped she hadn't overdone her pathetic trek to the house, but she'd wanted to impress upon him that showing his paintings mattered to her. In fact, she wasn't discouraged. She had complete faith in her ability to change his mind.

She could see it all now, as if it were displayed in neon lights on the study wall. The Town Hall, beautifully decorated and filled with festival shoppers, most of them lined up to see Ian's paintings. He'd stand modestly by with—with his agent. Yes, he'd have to get an agent.

Art dealers and national media would gravitate toward the festival, among the onlookers, taking notes, snapping pictures, filming.

Maybe she could talk Ian into growing a beard before the festival so he'd look more like an artist. A beret, she thought, was out of the question.

He'd become famous. Holman would be the next hot artists' colony. All she had to do was make him want to show those paintings. Couldn't be any harder than, say, winning the presidential election.

Tansy was so lost in her fantasy that when the phone rang, she answered it, forgetting it wasn't her phone. She did have the presence of mind to stammer, "Ian Foster's residence," instead of delivering a perky, "Hi!"

"Tansy, is that you?"

"Hey, Lilah," Tansy said. "Don't tell Ian I answered his phone, okay? It was a knee-jerk reaction, but he already doesn't like me and this might seal my fate."

Lilah laughed. "I'd like to say, 'Oh, no, he wouldn't mind at all,' but you're probably right, unless he's so keen on your getting his records in order that he's in the mood to forgive all."

"I don't think so," Tansy said, remembering his thundercloud expression as he repeatedly told her no.

"Actually, you were the one I wanted to speak to."

"Oh, good. What's up?"

"Well, first, the only topic of conversation in the valley is the festival."

"Whoo. We're talking about some big phone bills this month."

"And because of that, I've found you a spinner for Ian's booth. She works at the Haverstock Living Farm, and she's—let me see if I can get this straight—she's the school principal's sister-in-law's aunt's best friend."

"Then she's a shoo-in," Tansy declared. "That much family connection, she can't say no."

"I thought you'd be pleased to have another detail ticked off."

"I am." Tansy paused. "Lilah, speaking of ticked off, why does Ian seem so mad at the world all the time? He does nice things for people, but you'd never know it."

"It's just his way," Lilah said. The intimacy in her voice was gone, and she spoke lightly. "Don't let him scare you."

Tansy knew the subject was closed. "He doesn't scare me," she said, feeling irritable. "He annoys me."

Lilah snorted, sounding like herself again. "You and everybody else except his family. Okay, I'll let you get back to work."

Tansy hung up and drummed her fingertips on the desk. Ian had more than one secret, and Lilah, a close friend, wouldn't tell her what it was. It had to be big.

FROM THE WINDOW OF HIS OFFICE, Ian watched Tansy leave at five, then went into the house. The wince was already fixed on his face when he reluctantly opened the door to his office and the mess he knew he'd find inside.

It took him a minute to adjust. No mess. Only a neat stack of labeled folders lined up vertically in the same box he'd handed to her this morning. He read the top label, "Capital expenditures." That would be the new shearing equipment, or it had better be. He opened the folder to make sure. Yep, she got that part right anyway. He almost felt disappointed by the neat folders. He needed a reason to be mad at her.

He was too antsy to sit down at his desk. She was still *there,* somehow. Just a hint of a flowery scent hung in the air, and then the image of her running toward him this afternoon, so excited, appeared as if it were happening right in front of him, right now. And then the way she'd looked on her way back to the house.

He growled and stalked out of the room. "Edna," he said gruffly on the way past the kitchen door, "I'm going to the barn for a while. Call me when dinner's ready."

Instead of just saying okay, she turned toward him, beaming. "That Tansy Appletree is the nicest woman," she bubbled. "I knew she was a good mayor, but I had no idea—"

"It's an emergency," he said, and fled, but not fast enough to miss her deep sigh and a few muttered words he wasn't meant to hear. As rapidly as his feet could take him, he went into his studio, and, until Edna called, expressed everything that was in his heart in the only way he knew how to.

IAN WENT TO A LOT OF TROUBLE not to see Tansy the next day. He was out of the house and walking the meadows before nine, surrounded by bodyguards, which was how he was coming to think of Tim, Joe, and his hands. He invented a pressing need to leave during the lunch hour, which meant he had to make do with a sandwich at the Holman coffee shop, a far cry from one of Mike's Philly cheesesteak wonders, but if he went to Mike's Diner, he'd have to explain why he wasn't at home eating Edna's fabulous food, and Mike would lecture him on what an idiot he was being.

But as it turned out, he wasn't safe in Holman, either.

"Ian," Nettie said, bustling out with a BLT—burned toast, dubious tomato, bacon less cooked than the toast and lettuce too far gone to feel nostalgic for the vegetable patch in which it had been raised. "It's so nice of you to offer to do that wool booth at the festival!"

Offer? Before he could set her straight, tell her he'd been blackmailed, she'd sailed on. "It will be the hit of the festival. The kids will love it. And incidentally—"

"Ian!" A group of the church ladies—at least that's who he thought they were—zeroed in on him. "Aren't you the greatest to offer to help out with the festival." The one who was talking—he had no idea what her name was—leaned close. "My daughter is a fabulous knitter. Look at my sweater. Her work, something she did without any effort at all. You should see her masterpieces." She smiled proudly.

Ian looked. It was a sweater, for sure, and it was green with a high yellow content, a lot like the color he used for spring leaves twisted by a late storm. Looked a lot better on canvas than it did on her. "Mmm-hmm," he mumbled. He picked up his sandwich and got it within an inch of his mouth before another voice intruded.

"Marnie does do beautiful work," the second woman said, "but so does my daughter." She looked the first woman directly in the eyes and said, "She's won awards at many craft fairs. I can't quite remember whether Marnie—"

"You'll include crocheting, surely," said a third voice. "My mother's lap robes are exquisite."

Ian had had enough. He did the only thing he could think of. He whipped out his cell as if it had been vibrating in his pocket, flipped it open and feigned a look of desperation. Feigned? He *was* desperate, so he imagined he was pretty convincing. "No!" he said. "I'll be right there. Nettie," he called out, "gotta run." He put a ten-dollar bill on the table and raced for his truck, hearing Nettie's voice in the background saying something about a doggie bag. He wouldn't feed that sandwich to anybody's doggie.

Ian sneaked back onto his property—sneaked, when it was his home! He was starving, but couldn't go into the kitchen to beg a plate from Edna, because Tansy might still be having lunch. He couldn't even ask for food in his own home!

Feeling like a hunted man, he sought out Joe, Tim and the hands, ate their leftovers, thanking the powers that be for Edna's consistent overestimation of what six hungry men might eat, and didn't go back to the house until he saw Tansy's car zoom up his drive to the road.

It had to end. He couldn't endure his present situation long enough for Tansy to finish her work. He felt homeless, helpless, hungry—and mad, because he hadn't felt that way in a long, long time, and had thought he'd never have to feel that way again.

"DAMN YOU," TANSY YELLED at the top of her lungs when the computer froze yet again in the middle of an installation. She gave the monitor a slap it didn't deserve, because it was closer than the CPU.

It was no use. She'd added capacity to the computer so she could install more up-to-date programs—and not inexpensively—but the computer had glitches. Something was wrong with the hard drive. The computer was literally forgetting things, something she'd thought couldn't happen. It unexpectedly turned files into read-only files. It often froze, and all she could do was reboot, which worked until it froze again. She'd set it to save every thirty seconds so as not to lose anything, but she wasn't trying to write a document, she was trying to install a tax program. Because of the freezing, she'd had to start all over three times, and the third time had been the last straw.

She was dreading telling Ian he needed a new CPU, so before she did, Dr. Appletree would have to make a house call. She got down on the floor with the maddening machine and began to take it apart. She'd never done that before. It would be a learning experience, and, she told herself frankly, if she couldn't get it back together, so be it.

FROM THE MEADOW, Ian heard a shout come from the house. He couldn't distinguish the words, or tell if it was a cry of pain or fear, but it sure was loud. Remembering his own cry of pain when he opened the tax letter and Daniel's overreaction, he walked calmly toward the house.

Edna might have burned herself, or fallen down. He moved a little faster. Tansy might have electrocuted herself working on the computer. He broke into a run. He went to the kitchen first to see Edna upright, not nursing a burn, but flouring cubes of beef. "Did you hear somebody shouting?" he asked her, a little out of breath.

"It was Tansy," she said placidly. "My goodness, that girl has spirit, and a spicy tongue, too."

"What was she yelling at?"

"I don't know. Go ask her."

Just what he didn't want to do, but he supposed he should. He went down the hall to his office. The door was open, so he peered inside.

What he saw was the cutest bottom he'd ever seen, small but rounded in a way that made his mouth water, sending the blood rushing straight to his groin. Those curves were discreetly hidden beneath black slacks, but what was under the black slacks? he wondered. Besides skin as soft as lambswool, the color of cream. Did she have a faint sprinkle of freckles there, too, like the ones that bridged her tilted little nose? Modest cotton panties? Black lace? A scarlet thong?

His lustful thoughts faded somewhat when he saw his computer in pieces on the floor, with Tansy bent over the dismembered body as if she might have chopped it up herself. At least he'd stopped drooling, he hoped, when she straightened up and whirled to face him. She looked so mad her face was almost as orange as her sweater.

"Something happen?" he said, hearing the croak

that came from his throat and thinking that if she commented on it, he could tell her he had a cold.

She put her hands on her hips. "What happened," she said, "was a fight between me and this computer. It was winning, so I took it down."

Ian gazed at the pieces. "You're in better shape than it is. Are you sure you acted in self-defense?"

"The emotional damage this—this—geriatric case has done to me will scar me for the rest of my life."

A condition with which he was all too familiar.

"What?" she said. "What did I say? Have I actually hurt your feelings?" The fight went out of her. She looked worried.

He hadn't meant to let anything show on his face. Usually he handled that sort of thing brilliantly. He'd have to cover for it. "Of course you did. This computer and I have been together for years," he said sadly. "We made a commitment to each other. I can't bear to see it end."

A smile twitched at the corner of her mouth. A lovely mouth, smooth and glossy—and she'd gotten her "spirit and spicy tongue" back again. "Well, I'm sorry. You'll have to ask it for a divorce. Tell it I'm the other woman."

"It'll be a messy divorce," Ian said, looking at the pieces strewn across the floor. "It could make a lot of trouble for you."

"Nothing a broom and dustpan can't handle. Ian." She pointed at him, moving closer and closer in a way that could pass for threatening if she didn't look so cute. "This computer. Does. Not. Work. The modem seems to dislike the Internet. It hides files, or loses them altogether, how would I know? And it freezes up so often I couldn't get the tax software installed before it went off again!" She lowered her voice to a growl. "You *have* to buy a new one."

"Okay," he said, loving the surprise on her face. Tansy was inches away, gazing up at him, her lips parted. Ian's head was spinning. He was clearly not in his right mind because before he could stop himself, he lowered his mouth to hers and kissed her.

The first touch was like an electrical shock, a rush of recognition that he was a man, a hungry man, and she was a desirable woman. He expected her to push him away, but when she didn't, he relaxed into the kiss, savoring it. Her lips were even softer than he'd imagined, and he was amazed to feel them answering his with gentle pressure, her body leaning into his, warm and yielding. When she rested her hands on his arms, then slid them up to the nape of his neck, he was dizzied by the fuzzy sensation of growing desire.

Which he had to end. Immediately. What was he doing? What had brought this on? It scared him—no, terrified him. With some difficulty he let her go, extricated himself from arms that lingered on his and, badly shaken, turned on his heel and left the room.

Tansy staggered to the desk chair and collapsed. Her whole body zinged with sexual energy. If Ian had kissed her one second longer, she'd have pinned him to the floor—some spot on the floor not littered with computer parts—and had her way with him.

What a surprise! The last thing she'd ever have expected. But, oh, how she'd enjoyed it. That was a surprise, too. Her highest goal had been to make him like her, or at least not snarl at her.

She spun in the chair, feeling like a kid on a merry-go-round, excited, elated—and quite incapable of obsessing on Ian's desperate need for a new computer.

After what had just happened, how could she say, "Would you like me to pick it out for you?" instead of "Why did you kiss me?" and "Please let's do it again."

It didn't take a Mensa member to figure out that Ian wished he hadn't done it and would probably never, ever, do it again. How could she bring the mood back? There was a limit to the number of computers she could destroy.

She knelt on the floor. "I'm sorry," she said to the computer parts. "I meant well. Do you think I might actually get to be the 'other woman'? No, '*the* woman,' that's what I'd have to be."

Did she even *want* to be Ian's woman? Talk about a poor choice of spouse for a politician. She smiled. But if—well, she was sure she could change all that.

Or change her goals.

Ridiculous. One kiss, and she was thinking about sending her entire life plan down the drain.

No need to do that. A little fling with a knockout man wouldn't do any harm. Except that she wasn't a flinger. Being serially faithful had been born into her, and she was incapable of falling in love with B until she'd fallen out of love with A.

She'd been deeply in love several times. Twice in grade school, when she'd poured out her passion in valentines, on which she'd written, "I like you. Tansy

Appletree." Twice in high school, where love got a little more physical. More mature now, each time she broke up with the current beau she did so with vows that they'd remain friends forever. Just once in college, where love was a *lot* more physical, and that romance was a disaster. She'd been faithful, of course, and assumed incorrectly that he shared her values—until she heard that he was going to marry the head cheerleader because she was pregnant.

It still hurt a little, thinking about that. Maybe it was why she hadn't aggressively pursued marriage and babies, had just been happy to have good friends, her work and lots of activities. Ian might have been hurt, too. She had a feeling that if he ever fell for a woman, he'd fall hard, and if the woman didn't catch him, he'd break. Or maybe he was already broken.

A clock chimed in her head. How long had she been sitting here, not working? She couldn't charge Ian for a kiss and its aftermath.

She leaped up from the chair. Activity would be a distraction. "Edna," she said a minute later, "I need a broom and dustpan."

Chapter Five

It was a typical Appletree get-together, with everyone talking at once on totally different topics, and Tansy's niece and nephew wreaking havoc that nobody noticed because of the adult decibel level.

The only topic that got everybody's interest was politics. Tansy's father, Roger Appletree, was the state senator for Serenity Valley. Her brother, Basil, was building a framework for running for governor. Her sister Rosemary, mother of the two hellions, was a loyal volunteer at the grassroots level, recruiting a solid voter base for her father, her brother and one day, Tansy. Her sister Sage was an extraordinary fundraiser, positively Machiavellian in her pursuit of campaign funds. Basil's wife, Rosemary's husband, Sage's boyfriend and Tansy's mother, Priscilla, simply endured. When they'd hooked up with Appletrees, they'd done it with their eyes wide-open, knowing perfectly well what they were in for.

"Being mayor of Holman is a good start," Tansy's father was pontificating, "but you need to be making a decision for the long run."

"In the short run, have some more pork roast," Tansy's mother said.

"Let's get Basil into office first," Tansy said, happily accepting a juicy slice of the roast, "and then we'll think about me. Would you pass the potatoes, please?"

"It's never too soon," Basil said, annoyingly siding with her father. "I decided to be governor when I was in high school."

"I wish you the very best of luck," Tansy said placidly, "and maybe after one term, I'll run against you."

Her joke didn't go over well, so she tried another tack. "Pop, you should unseat the state representative to Congress. He's not that well entrenched yet."

"But I like him," Roger said. "He's doing a great job, and I'd much rather spend a legislative session in Montpclicr than in Washington."

"All good points," Priscilla said somewhat nervously.

Tansy couldn't imagine her mother anywhere but in Vermont. She'd taught in the Holman Elementary School for years, and was practically worshipped by students and parents alike. Her husband's absences in Montpelier were one thing. Long visits to the nation's capital, which provided the media with news of scandalous affairs and other sorts of misbehavior, was quite another.

Tansy looked fondly at her father. He wouldn't be unfaithful to her mother if the other woman paid *him*. Her mother must know that, but she also knew from the women's magazines she read at the beauty salon that a wife could never be too careful.

That's what Tansy wanted, a man she could trust to be faithful to her—and a man she wouldn't take her eyes off for a second. Her mind drifted to Ian. She had a feeling a woman's unfaithfulness would hurt him so deeply he might never recover from it.

Was that what had happened to him to make him so off-putting?

"...you're doing with Ian," she heard from a distance. "Is that going well?"

Quickly she caught up. "I'm working for him, not with him."

Her father frowned. "He's an odd bird. Don't let yourself get caught in any shady dealings. Soon as you told me you were getting his taxes in order, I wondered if he was trying to hide something."

"If he was trying to hide something," Tansy said distinctly, "I wouldn't tell you about it. But I'll bet you a box of homemade truffles that he's not trying to hide anything, just get his stuff in better order."

"I thought he had a degree in business," Basil said.

"He does," Tansy said. She realized she was starting to feel irritated. "But not in computer science. That's what I'm actually helping him with. Let me put it this way." She paused. "He has Windows 98."

The collective gasp irritated her even more. "It's not like a *sin*," she said. "We have plenty of people in the valley who don't use computers at all. I'm going to update his system, and then you can think of him as normal."

"Do you know what makes him so reserved and grumpy?" Priscilla asked in her sympathetic voice. "He's not a bit like his brothers."

"No," Tansy said, "and it's none of my business."

"Somebody must have hurt him really badly," Rosemary said, ignoring Tansy's obvious wish to change the subject. "Has he ever dated anybody around here?"

"Not that I know of," Sage chimed in. "Sacha did her best to strike up a relationship with him last year, but it was no go."

"I don't know, Tansy," her father said, "that you should get involved with a man with something to hide. You have your political career to think of."

She'd had it. In a clear, cold voice, she said, "I'm *working* for Ian. What I'm *involved* in is the festival. Let's talk about that."

One of the nice things about her family was that women were not only allowed to be strong-minded, it was demanded of them. "Indian pudding, anyone?" her mother said brightly, and everyone at the table began to chatter just as brightly about the festival.

TANSY HADN'T EVEN TRIED to fathom why Ian was mad at her because he'd kissed her, but she *was* wondering how they'd left the matter of the new computer. His "Okay" before he kissed her didn't give her a whole lot of direction, and if it had, she'd have forgotten as soon as his mouth made contact with hers. It had been such a surprise, the shock of discovery, then the tenderness and then the surprising feeling that he might want more from her than a kiss. And most astounding of all was that her body was informing her with great enthusiasm that she wanted more, too.

Obviously, her intuition had been off yesterday. Ian had demonstrated by his sudden departure that he didn't want anything more from her than a presentation to a tax auditor.

But that didn't solve the problem of who was in charge of replacing the dead and decaying computer that waited for Ian's weekly trash pickup.

It would be more efficient for her to buy the computer, but suggesting that to him would mean talking to him, and she felt shy—Tansy Appletree, shy!—about talking to him right now. Maybe she'd feel braver tonight at home.

No, the first communication was up to him, she told herself stubbornly. In the meantime, she was spending the day at her office, catching up on her mayoral duties, which weren't many, and her festival plans, which were staggering.

TANSY HADN'T SHOWN UP at all today. Of course she couldn't work without a computer, but he imagined she was off somewhere plotting how to get him to show those paintings.

Frustrated beyond endurance, Ian made for his truck and set off for Daniel's house. If you absolutely had to have a soul talk with somebody, a rare event for Ian, Daniel was your best bet. Mike was just too optimistic. Too happy. Once the happiness had been a facade, his defense against the past, but now, sappily in love with Allie, he was happier than Ian could handle.

When it came to happy, Daniel himself was like a bear elbow-deep in honey. His home life with Lilah and all those boys was a sitcom. Like, perfect. In fact, Ian was starting to feel like a third wheel. Left out of the Happy Club.

Bull. He was happy enough just as he was. His family included him in more family gatherings than he'd like to be included in. He had his sheep, his escapes to the studio to paint—

Aargh. That's why he had to talk to Daniel. Daniel, however happy, had a balanced attitude. He could walk a fence without falling off. He'd present the pros and cons and suggest Ian think them over.

"Mike and I have been telling you to show your paintings for the last couple of years," Daniel said once Ian had arrived and bared his soul.

Ian blinked. What happened to that balanced attitude, those pros and cons? "But I don't want to," he said firmly. "They're amateurish. I painted them, I'm the one who gets to decide if anybody else gets to see them. Am I missing something here?"

"Yeah," Daniel said. "You may be an amateur, but your work isn't amateurish. It's good stuff. It's good because it comes from inside you, it's honest, it's the way you express the feelings you can't let out any other way."

Now Daniel was an art critic? He'd paused, stopped spouting nonsense, forever, Ian hoped, because all he'd wanted to hear was that he was right not to show his paintings. But Daniel's slow smile told him he wasn't off the hook yet.

"Your technique's not bad, either," he said. "In fact, your skill with the brush is a heck of a lot better than your skills with people. The attitude's still there—in Technicolor—but it's not aimed directly at anybody."

"Gee, thanks," Ian said. He had to sound sarcastic because Daniel had given him something to think about. He *could* put his deepest, darkest secrets on canvas. He didn't have to confide in anybody. His palette was his shrink, and a lot less expensive.

But *showing* those paintings to the world, even this small corner of the world, would be the same thing as publishing an autobiography!

Had love driven Daniel crazy? Didn't he realize what all the publicity could lead to?

"No," Ian said decisively. "I'm not showing the paintings."

Daniel muttered something he'd never say in front of his boys. "Okay. Have dinner with us, anyway."

"Is Tansy coming?"

"No."

"All right, I'll stay."

Daniel threw up his arms in resignation, then led Ian through the clinic door and into the noise and bustle of the house.

"Ian!" Lilah wiped her hands and gave him a hug and a peck on the cheek. "Stay for dinner?"

He had to admit it was pleasant to be greeted so warmly, to know he was always welcome. As big as Daniel's household was, he knew there was always enough food for one more—or six more. Now that he wasn't being counseled by his brother, he felt much more comfortable. "Thanks," he said. "An offer I can't refuse."

"How's Tansy doing?"

End of comfort. "Fine," he lied. "I'm getting a new computer."

"Amazing," Lilah said with a teasing tilt of her head. "If Tansy talked you into that, she could talk anybody into anything."

"Yeah."

"I caught a glimpse of her downtown this afternoon, running around like a whirling dervish, the way she always does. I guess she had to do some catching up on the festival, huh?"

"I guess." Daniel gave him an assessing look and Ian vowed to avoid being alone with him again this evening.

"We're almost ready," Jesse, a retired marine who'd become a member of Daniel's wildly extended family, announced. "Get out of my way and start sitting down."

The boys began to flow into the room. A little late, Nick bolted through the door. "Uncle Ian," he said, beaming as he slid into a chair. "I didn't know you were coming for dinner."

"He wasn't," Daniel said. "He came over to talk to me and I made him stay."

"What were you talking about?"

Ian considered the question for a second and decided Nick was too young to be told. "None of your business."

Daniel apparently disagreed. "We were talking about Uncle Ian's paintings," he said cheerfully, "and whether he ought to show them to other people."

Ian wanted to strangle him, but the look on Nick's face stopped him in his tracks. The boy was suddenly transformed. "You paint pictures?" he breathed.

"Yeah," Ian mumbled with a sharp glance at Daniel, who smiled serenely. "Just for fun."

"May I see them sometime?"

"Oh. Well. I don't know. They aren't very good."

"That's not true," Lilah protested. "They're wonderful."

"Nick is interested in art," Daniel said. "He'd like to see what you're doing."

Sure. Start with Nick. Then showing them to the whole world would be easy. Daniel and Lilah were ganging up on him. Had Tansy asked them to put on a little pressure? If she had, he could easily put her out of his mind, because he didn't like gossips. She'd found the paintings, but for all she knew, nobody else had found them and she shouldn't have told.

He was angry, but it wasn't Nick's fault. "Okay, I'll let you see them," he agreed, speaking only to the boy. "I'll pick you up Saturday morning. How's that?"

"Great! Thanks, Uncle Ian."

"I'll look forward to it," Ian said, and maybe he did.

He wasn't able to escape Daniel after dinner. "Are you and Tansy not getting along because she wants you to show your work at the festival? Was that why she was in town today instead of working on your taxes?"

"She was in town today because she can't work without a computer, and mine's beyond repair. I mean, like, she tore it to pieces and put it in the trash."

Daniel snorted. "Sounds just like her," he said. "So you're getting a new one at last?"

"Have to." He paused. Maybe he could use a little advice here. "We didn't exactly talk about whether she'd pick it out for me, or if I'm supposed to do it myself."

"Call her."

Ian ducked his head. "I sort of don't want to."

"Why? Oh, wait, I know. You've managed to make her mad at you."

"No, no, it's, well, I just think, I mean—" He couldn't think of a single lie, and no way would he tell Daniel he'd pounced on Tansy. It would make his brother far too happy.

Daniel didn't even protest. "Then e-mail her. You *do* e-mail, don't you?"

"Of course I do," Ian said, feeling thoroughly exasperated, "when, that is, I have a computer, which, at the moment—"

"Come on," Daniel said, motioning Ian to follow him to the living room. "I want to show you something. Look, a computer! Wait—look over there. By golly, a laptop. Two laptops." He turned to face Ian. "So e-mail her. Now."

"I don't know her address."

"I have it," Lilah called from the kitchen. Did the woman have the ears of a bat?

Cornered, no options left to him, Ian sat down at the desktop and logged on to Web mail. Then he paused with his fingers poised over the keyboard.

"I'm not going to stand here watching you think about how to ask her in the most unlovable way," Daniel said. "I'll check out the homework situation and come back."

Five, six, seven minutes later, Ian had drafted a suitable message. "I would appreciate it if you'd choose the new computer and a new monitor."

He hadn't started with "Dear Tansy," or "Hi, Tansy," or even, "Tansy, listen up!" but the words looked a little stark sitting there, so after thinking it over carefully, he added, "Ian."

"Finished?" Daniel was in the hall and coming toward him, so Ian clicked Send really fast and went off-line. If Daniel started editing, the e-mail would turn into a love letter.

"Yes," he said, "and it's time for me to be going."

HOME FOR TANSY WAS HER little apartment, which she loved. The second she was out of school, she informed her parents that grown-ups didn't live with their families. No, she'd told them, their carriage house apartment would be just like living in the house.

After a lot of networking, she'd snagged the carriage house apartment of an elderly woman who was nearly blind and even more nearly deaf. Tansy recognized that her choice might indicate she'd been thinking about having a love life someday, and had chosen privacy above all. She could easily buy a tiny house now, after five years of a successful accounting practice, but she liked it here, and you could never save too much money. Life had too many rainy days—and in Vermont, they were more likely to be snowy and icy.

And besides, something not written into the lease was that Tansy called her landlady three times a day, and if she didn't get an answer, she knocked on the door, then used the key, ready to call 911.

Which was silly, because the woman's children checked on her constantly. But she couldn't help herself.

All in all, it was a win-win arrangement. Now Tansy was cuddled in a cozy armchair with a little desk pulled up to it, a cup of cocoa on the side table, making lists while her chicken—dinner for three nights minimum—roasted in the oven.

A list of the committees she'd need to form to get the festival arranged. A list of potential committee heads. A list of possible committee members.

About a thousand people lived in Serenity Valley, and while the benefit was intended to support the Holman Town Hall, the valley operated as a unit. So a thousand, subtract the children, then consider that the women were more likely to get involved in the festival—sad, but true—and she had about a hundred-fifty people who should be asked to serve on a committee.

Many of them would refuse. Too many desperately poor people lived in the valley and were supported to the extent of the state's resources, but Tansy had decided that everyone should be invited to participate. This wasn't a New York benefit event, it was a community effort.

Deep in thought, she answered the phone absent-mindedly, then said, "Allie! Hi!" Allie was Mike Foster's fiancée. Tansy and Lilah had become Allie's closest friends in the valley.

"I'm calling for a life and death purpose," Allie said.

Tansy might have panicked if Allie had sounded equally panicked, which she didn't.

"Mike wants us to chair the festival food committee," Allie went on, "in fact, he's a little frantic about it. Don't worry—no weird food, but he wants to make sure what we're offering to outsiders is top quality. He'll accept donations, of course—if he approves of them."

"I'm thrilled," Tansy said. Mike's Diner was *the* place to eat in the valley, and one of the few attractions to outsiders. She'd include the restaurant name in the flyers she'd distribute—she mentally added "Publicity Committee" to her list—and newspaper ads she intended to run. It would pull in some of those outsiders. "I can stop worrying about the food, then. Do you think he could make a few concessions, like Gertrude's piecrust you could pave a road with?"

"No," Allie said with a smile in her voice, "but he can tell Gertrude that she's already done so much for the community that she deserves a rest. And if that doesn't work, he'll price the pie accordingly."

"Quarter a slice, max, including a scoop of ice cream," Tansy said. "The food committee is all yours, and I appreciate it so much."

"*Mike* will appreciate it so much," Allie said. "Last night he had a nightmare about going to the festival and finding there was nothing to sell but bologna-and-cheese sandwiches on white bread." Without even a break, she added, "How are you and Ian getting along?"

Nope, I'm not confiding in his family. "Just fine," Tansy said.

"Is it true you talked him into a new computer?"

"Not exactly. I demolished the old one, so he didn't have another option."

Allie giggled and soon ended the call. Tansy gleefully added in their names under "Food Committee" and crossed that worry off her list. The delicious scent of browning chicken filled the air, so she shuffled into the little kitchen alcove in her fuzzy slippers and arranged a plate for herself.

Her life was so simple. The low lady's desk she'd found in an antiques shop, which rolled around easily on its original ceramic casters, was exactly big enough for a laptop and a dinner plate. While she ate, her thoughts went back to Ian and his computer. Wouldn't hurt to do some comparison shopping.

Between bites, she went to the Web sites of the two brands she trusted most. She knew, more or less, what Ian needed. The new computer would come with updated programs. She'd have to teach Ian how to use them. It would take hours and hours—her mouth watered thinking about sitting with Ian, looking over his broad shoulder, having a legitimate reason to stare at his profile as long as she wanted to.

Unless he still wasn't speaking to her.

She sighed. Half an hour later, she'd priced the equipment directly from the manufacturers, compared the costs with those of a discount dealer in New York, and had armed herself to talk to a local dealer first, when she had Ian's permission.

Before she put on her warm flannel granny gown and climbed into the high, soft bed, she'd take a second to check her e-mail.

Ian's message popped out at her as if it were on springs. "I would appreciate it if you'd..."

She read it three times, then began to laugh. She laughed until tears ran down her cheeks. In bed with a good book to read, she occasionally started laughing again, quite inappropriately, since the book was so sad she'd almost decided to return it to the library unread.

He'd used somebody else's computer, of course, so there wasn't much point in answering the e-mail, but she couldn't resist. Sliding out of bed, she quickly clicked on Reply and wrote, "Certainly," then got the giggles again, and again, and again.

Chapter Six

From a window in the barn, Ian followed the progress of Tansy's car as she made her way up the driveway. When it went out of his line of view, he stewed for a few minutes, then went back to work. If she needed to talk to him, she'd have to come out and find him.

When she didn't, he began listening for her car to leave. That didn't happen, either.

Curiosity was driving him crazy. Unable to work, he asked Tim if he could use his computer to check his e-mail. He was ashamed by his excitement when he saw Tansy had answered his post, and he opened it quickly.

"Certainly," it read. *Certainly?* Unlike him, she hadn't even signed her name. For a second or two, he felt hurt. Then he felt a smile coming on. She was one tough lady. Maybe that's what he needed, a strong woman who could give back as good as she got.

Of course he did. He needed her to get him through this audit.

It was close to seven when he heard her drive away. He'd been hiding out in the barn, in his studio, actually, but now he could safely go into the house.

He heard his employees milling around in the living room, talking about the weather while they waited for dinner. They all ate together at the round table in the dining room. It was easier on Edna to feed them in the main house instead of the bunkhouse. He gave them a wave, and went to the kitchen.

Edna greeted him with her hands on her hips. "And where have you been? I thought you might have died out there. Tansy's already gone, wouldn't stay for dinner, everybody's starving, the chicken's dried out…"

"Um," Ian said, "I got busy. I was painting." What he didn't admit was that he was hiding.

The people who worked for him were family, too. They knew about his hobby and were such big fans that it made him uneasy, as if they were relieved he had something other than them to take out his grumpiness on.

Edna's eyes softened. "Dinner'll be ready in ten or fifteen minutes. I was waiting to see the whites of your eyes before I finished things up." She paused. "The mail's in your office. By the time you take a look at it, the food will be on the table."

It sounded like an order, but he always went to his office when he came back from work. He obeyed the order, sat down at his desk and found himself staring at a slender monitor instead of the one he'd owned this morning. A note was taped on the monitor. Do Not Touch.

He peered under the desk. She'd somehow gotten the new computer this morning. Interesting. He sat back in his chair, contemplating the implications of her terse message. Don't touch it because if you do it will blow up? Tansy was strong, but he hadn't thought of her as violent—well, until she massacred the old computer. Don't touch it because she'd started something on it he might interrupt? She'd left the thing on, but he couldn't see anything on the monitor that indicated an installation in progress. On the other hand, how would he know? The only thing he'd ever installed was a new printer, which he bought only because the old one wouldn't print anymore, and he was ready to fling it out the window before it finally congratulated him on having success-fully installed it.

What he saw was his desktop looking exactly the way it had looked before. *Who does she think she is to tell me not to touch my new computer!* Defying the note, he looked for his e-mail program icon, and there it was. So he opened it, and it welcomed him into its close circle of friends, just as it always did.

He clicked on New Mail, then, just to see what hap-pened, opened Address Book. Amazingly, there was her e-mail address.

So he wrote, "What do you mean I can't touch my own computer? I touched it, and it and I are still alive."

And deleted it. Then he wrote, "Tell me how to pay for it."

And deleted it.

"Ian," Edna called from the kitchen, "we're ready."

Under pressure, he typed, "Thank you. Tell me who to pay."

Delete, delete. And then, "Thank you. Please let me know where to send the check. Ian." And clicked on Send before he got any more carried away.

AMAZING, TANSY THOUGHT when she opened the e-mail the next morning. The *thank you* and the *please* were dramatic breakthroughs. But she wouldn't hold her breath waiting for Ian to ask her how to use the tax program. She was the one who had to use the program first, had to get him ready for the audit.

Piece of cake.

When Tansy arrived at the farm the next morning, Edna ushered her into the office where the scents of coffee and cinnamon rolls swept her off her feet. She'd already had coffee and a full breakfast, but the cinnamon rolls were irresistible. With her mouth full, she got right to work transferring the organized documentation onto a spreadsheet.

She didn't see Ian all day. So what? She had a job to do, and she was doing it.

NICK'S YELL CARRIED ALL the way to the truck. "Uncle Ian's here! Bye!"

The boy was in the truck before Ian could get out of it. His eyes were sparkling, his cheeks were flushed from the cold November air and his obvious excitement. Ian had a strange sensation that Nick belonged in his truck, that his affection for the boy went a little deeper than the fondness he felt for the rest of Daniel's boys, which he worked so hard to hide.

He couldn't help himself. He smiled at Nick, and Nick sent back a wide grin of pure happiness. "Ready for a visit to the museum?" he asked.

"Uncle Daniel said to call it a studio," Nick said. "Is that right? Were you kidding when you called it a museum?"

"Yeah." He gave Nick another smile. If he kept this up, he was going to strain the muscles in his cheeks. "Your art doesn't end up in a museum unless it's really, *really* good."

"Where does it end up?"

On a bonfire. "Well, sometimes a public place like a restaurant, or a library, or a hospital will let you hang your paintings there." Mike had been bugging him to fill up the restaurant walls. Ian had claimed ruined appetites as his reason for refusing. "That's victory number one."

"What's two?"

"That a gallery owner likes what you do and offers to sell your stuff in his shop. That's bigtime, Nick, selling a piece of art. The museum comes last, after you've sold a whole lot of stuff and a really picky expert says something of yours *belongs* in a museum."

How had he spouted all this so easily? Not just the words, which he thought might be the most he'd ever said at once, but the career-building part? Had he actually been thinking that one day he might…

Naw. Ridiculous.

But Nick was talking, and Ian wasn't listening, which wasn't a good thing for a kid, especially one as needy as Nick.

"…teacher likes what I do in class. I made a lamb out of what she called pop-e-ay mash-ay, and she gave me an A."

"A lamb, huh?"

"Yeah." Nick paused. "If you put my lamb in your living room, that'd mean I'd taken the first step, right?"

"You're right. I could put it on that table by the front door. Everybody who came in—" they'd be the same people, day after day, week after week "—would see it before they saw anything else. I have a better idea, though. I bet Uncle Mike would put it next to the cash register in the restaurant. A lot more people would see it there."

Nick thought about it. "I'd like it better in your house," he said.

Ian's voice was a little gruff when he said, "Thanks. I'll take good care of it."

He was actually having a conversation. The other person would talk, then he would talk, then the other person would talk—he shook his head. It took a seven-year-old boy to get him talking. That was pathetic.

"Here we are," he said, feeling nervous when he saw Tansy's car parked in the drive. "Edna's got some hot chocolate ready for you, and then we'll go to the studio."

Oh, wow. Ian couldn't express how much he didn't want to go into the house. What was Tansy doing here on Saturday, anyway? She needed time off like everybody else, and he needed time off from hiding in the barn.

He had to be brave, though, because Nick had to have Edna's hot chocolate. On the way in, stepping softly and closing the door silently, he showed Nick where the lamb would sit, then took him into the kitchen.

"Hello, there, young man," Edna said. "I've been looking forward to seeing you. Sit right here and I'm going to give you the best cup of hot chocolate you've ever had. You, too," she said to Ian, in not half as friendly a voice.

What had he done? He'd told Edna he was bringing Nick out to the farm. She'd said, "That precious boy. I'll give him hot chocolate, then lunch…"

But Tansy was here now and Edna had scruples. She wouldn't invite Tansy to join the hot-chocolate moment unless Ian told her to. And he hadn't, because he'd had no idea Tansy would be here on a Saturday.

Still, Edna had clearly expected him to see Tansy's car, then say something like, "Tansy's here. She might like to say hello to Nick, sit down with us for hot chocolate," but he hadn't. Now she was mad at him for not seeing what his next step should be.

The bottom line was that Ian's house was no longer his castle. He guessed he'd have to live with it until the audit was over, but then, by God, he'd get right back up on his throne and make it clear that he was the king.

"I'm done, Uncle Ian," Nick said while Ian still brooded. "This was great," he said to Edna. "Thanks."

"Chicken pot pie for lunch," she said, smiling at him broadly.

Tansy had stayed away from the kitchen, so that was a relief. After he'd had a second or two of relief, he began to worry about what Nick would think of his paintings. They weren't for kids. They were sort of scary. Obviously, Nick had known a lot of fear in his short life. He didn't need to be exposed to any more.

Relieved, anxious…he was just a whirlpool of emotions this morning, wasn't he? If Nick hadn't been with him, he would have rested on the barn stoop and put his head in his hands for a few minutes. He wanted things to go back to being exactly as they had been.

It was all the fault of the IRS. His present turmoil had begun the minute that damned letter arrived.

"Here it is," he said to Nick, and led him through the door and down the stairs. At the bottom, Nick stopped and simply stared.

The boy was silent for such a long time, staring at first one painting then the next, seeming to examine every detail, that Ian became concerned. "Want to see the paints and brushes?" he asked.

"Sure," Nick said. His feet moved, but his head swiveled back to the paintings.

"It's okay," Ian said gently. "Take as long as you want."

At last, Nick turned to him. "Uncle Ian, were you mad when you painted these pictures?"

The question startled Ian speechless. "I, um, well, I..." He suddenly realized what an enormous responsibility he had for this boy. He couldn't brush him off. He had to give whatever he had inside himself, openly and honestly. "I think maybe I was feeling mad," he said, "because sometimes I do. Do you?"

"Not as much as I used to."

"I'm not as mad as I used to be, either."

"Does painting help you not feel mad?"

Ian sighed. "I think so. Daniel thinks being mad helps the paintings, too."

"I was mad when I drew this." Nick pulled a folded piece of paper out of his back pocket and shyly handed it over.

Ian studied the crayon sketch. It pierced his heart. Miles and lifetimes away from a papier-mâché lamb, this wasn't beautiful, sweet or childish. It was compelling, drawing him into Nick's nightmares—or maybe to the real nightmare of Nick's mysterious past. And the picture told him that the child's life had once been chaotic, even terrifying.

It made him sick. His life had been like that, too, and the sorrow he felt for himself was trivial compared with his anger toward parents who would offer a life like that to a boy like Nick.

Nick waited, looking worried. Ian nodded and said quietly, "Good work, buddy. Spend the afternoon here, and we'll start getting that down on canvas."

The look in Nick's eyes—relief? Gratitude?—was like a gift, the best gift Ian had ever gotten.

SHE WAS JUST LIKE THE ELDERLY ladies of Holman, Tansy grumbled at herself, the ones who spent a significant amount of time each day peering through their curtains at the neighbors, hoping they might do something worth gossiping about. She had, in fact, been looking through Ian's wooden blinds while she waited for yet one more software program to install when Ian and Nick headed to the barn, and she was simply crazy with curiosity. She'd almost followed them, using the excuse of wanting to say hi to Nick, but something—her last shred of good manners, she imagined—held her back.

Ian could just be giving Nick some time with the lambs, or he might be showing the boy his paintings. But how could a seven-year-old, even a smart and sensitive one like Nick, understand those paintings?

This weird standoff with Ian that started not with a fight, but with a kiss, had gone on long enough. She had to run into him by "accident." An accident she'd plotted and caused to happen.

It wasn't easy to get anything done while she ran back and forth to the windows, but she was thinking about the bigger picture and she wouldn't charge Ian for the morning. At last, he and Nick emerged from the barn. When she'd determined that he wasn't taking Nick back to the truck, that he was bringing him into the house, she timed her movements, and at precisely the moment the front door opened, she went down the hall toward the kitchen.

"Nick!" she exclaimed. "Great to see you."

Nick ran to her and gave her a hug. She picked him up—not easy for somebody her size—and turned the hug into a squeeze. "Tansy, guess what?" he said, looking excited enough to burst. "Uncle Ian showed me his paintings!"

"That's great," she said, afraid to look at Ian, knowing he was probably fuming. "Do you like them?" It was a safe question. It was clear he was delighted with everything about life this morning.

"Yeah," he breathed, "and I showed him one of my pictures, and he said I could turn it into a painting and he'd show me how!"

Tansy prided herself on her powers of persuasion, but she'd tried very hard to draw a line between persuasion and manipulation. *Well, forget about it. I'm tossing that one out of my value system for now, and manipulate the heck out of Ian.*

"You know," she said, taking Nick's hand and turning her back on Ian, "I've been trying to convince Ian that he should display his work." She ignored the sharp intake of breath she heard over her shoulder. "I thought the festival—you know about the festival?" When Nick nodded enthusiastically, she went on. "I thought it might be a good place to start."

"That's what Uncle Daniel said, too," Nick contributed. He paused, but seemed to be thinking, so she didn't interrupt. "Would he be able to sell a painting there?"

"Oh, yes," Tansy said, "and he only has to contribute ten percent to the festival." She was trying to transmit some additional information through Nick.

Nick's eyes were shining even more brightly. "So it would be like a gallery?"

"Well..." Tansy said, not quite knowing where this was going.

Nick whirled toward Ian. "You'd be starting at step two!"

Huh?

"Come on, Uncle Ian, you have to!"

Ian knew a trap when he saw one, and he usually saw it before, not after, he fell into it.

He hadn't fallen. He'd been shoved!

Tansy had obviously figured out that Daniel's boys were his soft spot and that he and Nick had some kind of special understanding. She couldn't know the reason—that he'd once been where they'd been, and if Daniel had been his foster father then, he'd be a different person now. But she knew enough, and she was using it against him.

"We'll talk about it," he said stubbornly.

"Can we talk about it while we're eating? Tansy, are you going to eat with us?"

"Well…" Tansy said.

Hell, no, Ian thought.

"Of course she is," Edna called out from the kitchen in her Queen Victoria voice.

"It's ready right now, so sit down before it gets cold." Herding Nick and Tansy into the kitchen and sitting around the table, he had thoughts about firing Edna, but then he'd lose Joe, too, and, face it, some pretty good food.

He thought Nick was innocent, but the kid sure was presenting a strong case. "I know it's scary to show other people what you've done," Nick said, so earnestly that he had to be sincere. "It scares me to show my teacher, but she always tells me if it's good, and sometimes she tells me how to make it better."

"Did you show this to her?" Ian held up Nick's crayon sketch.

"Yes, and she said it was really special."

Tansy was listening to them, her head moving slowly toward whoever was talking. She was quieter than Ian had ever seen her, as if she were caught up in a spell. So he was startled when she spoke.

"That's what makes a painting good, isn't it? That it's special. That it's something only one person could have painted, because the artist's heart is on the canvas. And yes, it's scary to show somebody your heart."

It sounded as if Tansy had decided to give up on her plan, that she finally understood what made him so stubborn about keeping his paintings private. He was afraid to show them.

Ian sat up straight in his chair. The hell he was. He

wasn't afraid of anything! He'd show her, and make Nick happy at the same time!

"All right," he said, hiding his anger at Tansy for thinking he was a coward. "I'll show the paintings at the festival."

The heavy silence in the kitchen made him realize what he'd done. He'd just given in, and when he was doing it, he'd thought it was his own idea!

He shot a glance at Tansy. She returned it straight on, then smiled.

Ian couldn't help himself. He smiled back.

Chapter Seven

"It's so cold out there," Tansy said to Edna, shivering as she made her way into the warmth of Ian's house on Monday morning. "I've lived here all my life. You'd think I'd be—"

"No time to chitchat," Edna scolded her. "Get in there and help him before he blows up the new computer."

Tansy raced down the hall to the office. "I told you not to touch it!" she cried.

"A simple letter to a textile company!" Ian raged. "That's all I wanted to do. And I can't find anything! There's no File, or Edit, or Format menu. There's no—"

"It's a new program," Tansy said soothingly. "I'll teach you how to use it."

"You have five minutes," he said, glowering at her. "This has to go in the mail today."

"It'll take longer than that," Tansy assured him, thinking of those hours and hours of instruction she'd been looking forward to and wondering if they were going to be any fun, after all. "I'll finish typing the letter for you, then when you have time, we'll—"

"I want my old program back."

"I'm afraid you can't have your old program back. New computers have the new program. I doubt that I could even find a copy of the old one to install. You have no choice but to move into the twenty-first century."

"Why, when the old program works just fine, do they have to dream up another one?"

"To make it better?"

Ian snorted. "It's not better. It's impossible to use. I wrote the letter already, I just can't format it. Look at it. I printed it in case I had to send it this way."

Tansy looked at his printout. The default font was small and a little bit artsy. The text was lined up along the left, as it should be, and he had managed to insert spaces between the paragraphs. When she saw how much information he'd imparted in so few words "—Adjust the invoice of August 19 to reflect our conversation of November 22, Sincerely—" she stifled another bout of the giggles, but the end result was two lines scrunched up at the top of the page. No, it wasn't a presentable business letter.

"I'll fix it," she promised him. "You go do something else. I haven't gotten around to setting up the program for you with icons you can find easily, so I'll do that this morning." She gazed at him sadly. "I should have bought you a Mac. Lots of people prefer them because they're very user-friendly. Many schools have chosen to use Macs. Even preschoolers use them. But since you already had a PC, I assumed—"

"I'm not a child," he growled. "You think I can't learn a new program? I can and I will." He paused, and Tansy leaped into the silence.

"I'm happy to teach you," she said humbly. She'd

manipulated him again and felt sort of bad about it, but in both cases, Ian had been acting like his own worst enemy—and somebody had to save him from the enemy.

He stood, staring at her. "You wear orange a lot," he said.

Talk about a non sequitur. Tansy glanced down at her orange turtleneck. "Orange is supposed to look good on redheads," she explained, "and besides, not many people like the color, so I get some great bargains."

His gaze burned into her. She was afraid to move, and he didn't come toward her. He said, uncommonly politely, "I'll see you later, then. At lunch."

He'd invited her to have lunch with him! Now she felt confident it was all right to say, "Maybe at five we could spend an hour figuring out the new program."

"I could be free at four, I think," he said, surprising her with his acquiescence. Then she noticed the hunger in his eyes, and desire danced through her. She wanted to put her arms around him and tell him he could kiss the breath out of her if he wanted to, but it wasn't time yet.

He would know the right time, and she'd wait for him. She knew he'd kiss her again someday.

"Better get to work." He pulled his gaze away from her, then glanced at his wrist, where his watch didn't seem to be, and frowned.

"Me, too," Tansy said. "I'll see you at noon."

Ian left then, but not angrily. In fact, he waved from the doorway. In just a few minutes he'd been transformed from a furious man to a calm and peaceful, nearly normal one. Tansy wouldn't ask herself what had happened. She'd just count her blessings.

IAN HAD FELT MORE RELAXED yesterday and had slept better last night than he had in years. Trying to write that letter this morning had frustrated the heck out of him, but didn't everybody get frustrated when a machine didn't work?

But then, when Tansy had barreled into his office in that silky, tight-fitting orange turtleneck, looking like a summer sunset, he'd felt himself calming down. Oh, yeah, he had to hide it for a while as a matter of pride, but he was thinking, *Tansy's here. She can fix everything.*

Why did that make him feel better? He'd have to think that one over. In the meantime, he actually did have work to do.

Joe caught him just as he entered the barn. "The boiler's on the blink again," he said.

"Buy a new one," Ian said distractedly.

"Rayford wants to know if you need any more help," Tim signed when Ian and Joe stepped into his office. "His brother just lost his job. He's got three kids."

"Hire him," Ian signed back.

Tim's eyes widened ever so slightly. After a pause, he signed, "We have another drinker in the bunkhouse."

"Reform him. I'm a little busy this morning. I'll let you guys handle everything." He turned to Joe. "And shop for a new boiler."

It was like a siren's call, his need to go to the studio. Convinced he'd left his business in perfect order, Ian went there immediately.

THERE WAS TENSION at the lunch table, but not enough to have the slightest effect on Tansy's appetite. Feeling they'd crossed a barrier, she chattered happily about Ian's new computer, town gossip, and the festival. From him she got nods and the occasional slight smile.

Until he blurted out, "How were you thinking of showing these paintings?"

He actually cared. She was touched by that. In fact, she'd been thinking about it a lot, and had come up with a plan. She rested her chin on her hand and said, "My first idea was to put you right out in the center of the room with the 'sheep to sweater' demonstration, but it would be hard to display the paintings. So now I think we'll put your booth in the center at the back and fill the wall with the paintings. They'll be the first thing people will see as they're coming through the door. How many pieces do you have?"

"I was sort of figuring that out today."

He "sort of" looked as if he was sorry he'd brought up the topic, and he didn't answer her question.

"Whatever, we'll hang them and tack a price tag beneath each one—"

"Do we have to put price tags on them?" He sounded nervous.

"Well, no, we could number them and have a corresponding list of prices for people to look at."

"It's the prices themselves that bother me, not how you do it. Couldn't I just leave it open and wait to see if anybody even wants one of them?"

Tansy couldn't let herself smile, so she quickly forked up a big spoonful of homemade macaroni and cheese and stuffed her mouth with it. "I'll find an art dealer to help us with the pricing—in case anybody wants to buy one."

"Just so it's not too much."

"I promise. Not too much."

Ian ducked his head toward the table. "How are the festival plans shaping up?"

My goodness, he was making an effort to show an interest! "Wonderfully," she said, "with a few problems. Nobody wants to chair the Publicity Committee." She might have to *be* the Publicity Committee, which wouldn't necessarily be a bad thing. She already knew how she wanted to advertise in a way that would bring all of Vermont to taste the pleasures of a tiny town in a hidden valley.

"You should think of a couple of people you know would do a good job and tell them to do it," Ian suggested. "That will solve your problem."

Tansy smiled. "Ian, I can't just tell people that they have to be in charge of the publicity. It wouldn't be right."

He seemed to consider what she said carefully because he didn't say a word for a few minutes, just stared at his plate. Then he raised his head. "You can persuade them. You're very good at that."

Oops. He'd noticed. He didn't say the words. He didn't have to. They both knew what he was thinking, and it had been nice of him not to come right out and say, "You can con them, just the way you conned me."

But she refused to feel bad about how she'd *persuaded* him to participate in the festival. It was good for him. Already he was opening up and having real conversations. She liked talking with Ian very much and, frankly, couldn't see how her persuasion had done him any harm.

"You're right. I guess I am good at that," she said,

turning her attention back to her plate. "Maybe I can think of someone I can persuade to help."

"Trust me. They won't stand a chance," he said, and gave her a quirk of a smile.

The smile was so unexpected and enticing that Tansy found herself laughing. Ian looking happy was something she could get used to really fast.

"WELL, THAT'S JUST DUMB." And so was he. Ian had been watching the time all afternoon, waiting for four o'clock, when he'd get his first lesson from Tansy about using the new computer programs. And now that he was here, she was the one who was driving him crazy, not the program.

"It *is* different," she said, "but you're getting it."

She sat beside and a little behind him so that he could be at the keyboard, but she could see what he was doing. Her light, flowery scent wafted over him, making him want to turn around and sink his face into her shoulder. Her arm brushed his when she pointed to something on the monitor screen, and her face was close enough to kiss.

He was losing it, that's what he was doing, under the stress of being in close quarters with a lovely woman after not associating with anyone but his family and his employees for years.

"What next?" he said gruffly, wanting to latch on to something that would stop him from thinking about sex.

"I think you can write a document now, don't you?"

The words puffed into his ear, and a zing shot straight down his body. "Probably." He could barely get the word out.

"So let's switch to the tax program. We won't have

much time to work on it, but I could give you an overview. Click on..."

There it was, all laid out before him, the possibility of one digital spreadsheet instead of two accounting books. He had to admit it—this would be good. Tansy's voice was soft as she explained that he'd be doing the work all at once, that the program would subtotal each time he made an entry.

When she drew closer to him, Ian's breath quickened. He realized he wasn't listening to her, that his mind was on nothing but her mouth, her scent, her small body he wanted so badly to hold.

"...all right," she said.

"Sorry..."

"It's all right to kiss me."

The shock made him whirl toward her. Her lips parted, and he accepted the gift she gave him.

He met her kiss, drew back, then brushed her mouth again with his. She accepted his touch willingly, then eagerly. Her hand went to his face, cupped his chin, pulled him deeper into the pain and pleasure of desire.

When he lifted her from her chair and put his arms around her, his need was so great that he had to hold back, press her gently to him, caress her lightly, until it was apparent that she wanted more. She crushed herself against him, her arms circling him, stroking his back with a rhythm so maddening that he couldn't wait any longer.

Heat filled him, suffocated him. Breaking away, he teased her lips with his tongue, buried kisses in her small, perfect ears, reveled in the sound of her soft moan. Desperately needing to touch her, he slid his hands beneath her sweater. His hands closed on skin as soft as velvet, and he quivered when he felt her tugging his shirt out of his trousers, touching his skin, too, sliding up and up, until he couldn't take much more without whisking her up into his arms and carrying her off to his bedroom—past the kitchen, where Edna would be cooking dinner.

Although he cast a longing glance over Tansy's shoulder at the sofa in the study, then checked the door to be sure it was closed, Ian faced the reality that they weren't alone. The heaven he wanted to share with her couldn't happen here and now.

Slowly and carefully, he pulled back. Tansy's eyes were closed, her lips swollen, her face flushed. He didn't want to let her go, but he had to—for now.

"Don't you dare run away," she whispered, still not opening her eyes.

He buried his smile in her soft, springy hair. "I'm through with running away," he said.

"Well, good, because I'm fed up with it."

He gripped her face in his hands. "You are one bossy woman, Tansy Appletree," he said.

"Yep," she answered, at last letting go of him, "and the sooner you learn it, the better."

"Ian!" It was Edna calling from the kitchen. With none-too-steady hands, he shoved his shirt back into his waistband and smoothed his hair. "You two about finished in there? Dinner's almost ready."

"Yes," he called back, so filled with joy he almost felt like laughing, "we're through for today. Be there in a minute." And to Tansy, he said, "Stay for dinner?"

"Oh, I couldn't bear to," she said, her voice still

whispery. "One second of me sitting at the table with you and we might as well advertise in the paper that we've reached the kissing stage."

"You're right," he said, because she was. His physical state was even more visible than hers.

"See you tomorrow?"

"Absolutely."

It was so sweet to see her breasts rise as she put on her coat, her nipples taut beneath the silky turtleneck, so wonderful to return the smile she sent him, and so hard to let her go out that door.

THANKSGIVING CAME AND WENT, a veritable tsunami of too many people and too much food. Not too many people for Tansy, but she could just imagine how Ian felt. In fact, he'd told her how he felt when she'd found an excuse to dash to Daniel's house for a few minutes of total bedlam that made her parents' house seem like being in church.

"I vant to be alone," he'd muttered, "vit you."

The next week went by in a haze of sidelong glances, stolen kisses and, yes, Ian's taxes. At times Tansy had to convince herself that they had any importance whatever, but, in fact, she had to be ready for that audit, and she would be armed to the teeth.

She smiled. Her biggest concern—why the brothers had formed the corporation—had faded away when she found the answer in the numbers. Each of them deposited all his earnings into the corporation account. Ian's income was far more than either of his older brothers', with Daniel's coming in second and Mike's trailing far behind. But every month, checks in identical amounts were deposited into their personal accounts. The Three Fosters, that's what they were. All for one and one for all.

It was one more reason to admire them. She knew that if anything bad happened to her, her brother, Basil, would sacrifice to help her out, but catch him dividing his legal partnership earnings with her? Not on your life.

Tansy would also be armed to the teeth for a successful festival. With the enthusiastic help of her assistant, Amy, and the help of half the town, the event was taking shape. She'd taken Ian's advice and convinced Selectperson Martha Latham that without her directing the publicity, they might as well give up on the entire idea of the festival.

Which, of course, freed up more time for Tansy to be with Ian. Time she really wanted. Each morning, excitement coursed through her veins as she drove to his house. Once safely inside his office, they'd steal a few precious kisses and caresses before she'd make him leave so she could get some work done.

Then she'd try to force herself to focus, which wasn't easy. She knew Ian was on the property, and her gaze kept drifting toward the window, wondering if he would walk by.

In her entire life, Tansy had never been this thrilled by a new relationship, if that was what they had. She wasn't sure. They kissed like two sex-crazed teenagers, but did they have more than that? She wasn't sure because they never talked about what was happening between them.

She was reluctant to say anything because she didn't

want to ruin what they had. If she tried to discuss it with Ian, she was fairly certain she'd lose ground. Ian just wasn't a talker. He'd never start the conversation, and she got the distinct impression that he was afraid she might. So she didn't question it, just reveled in the pleasure of it.

But she knew they couldn't go on like this forever. Sooner or later, she'd have to ask him where this was leading. But she couldn't do it here, not in her office with Amy eavesdropping, or at his house surrounded by people.

No, she needed to talk with Ian alone. Dinner seemed like the logical solution. She'd invite him to her apartment, cook something there and see where things led. Tansy glanced toward the window. She'd left the wooden blinds open so she could keep an eye on the barn. As soon as Ian returned to the house tonight, she'd ask him to come for dinner.

But not until she'd kissed him. A woman had to have her priorities straight.

"DINNER?" IAN FROWNED. "Why?"

"Because it would be fun," Tansy said, sliding her hands up his arms. "I'd like you to see my apartment. It would be fun to cook for you."

Ian didn't like the sound of this. Dinner meant being polite and talking. He didn't want to talk, especially not about what was happening between them.

"I don't know," he said, then reluctantly moved away from her. He'd let this thing between them go too far. He should have stopped it a long time ago.

Tansy laughed. "Ian, nothing bad is going to happen. It's just dinner."

"And talking." He pinned her with his gaze. "About us."

She shrugged. "Maybe. Or not."

Ian blew out a deep breath. "I know women need to talk about things like this."

"Not all women," she assured him. "I'm okay with the way things are. Well, for the most part. But we should meet somewhere besides your office for a change. My apartment seems like the logical choice."

Looking at her sweet smile, he realized he couldn't say no without having a reason. "What will I tell Edna?"

Her eyebrows peaked. "You have to ask Edna's permission to go out?"

"Of course not." Where was that reason? "She'll wonder, though, and might start other people wondering."

Her face got that thinking look. "Tell her," she said, "that we're trying out the chili Mike wants to serve at the festival."

Ian gave in. Might as well. He knew he would sooner or later. And the thought of being alone with Tansy was seriously tempting him. If he kept her mouth shut by keeping his on it the whole evening, maybe he could avoid that talk. "When?"

"Tomorrow night." Tansy took a step toward him, then the sudden banging on the door to the office made them both jump.

Ian muttered a curse and yanked the door open. Edna stood on the threshold. Selectperson Martha Latham stood behind her. Flanking Martha were a perky little blonde woman with a notepad and a man with a camera.

"Sorry to bother you," Edna said, her sharp gaze darting from Ian to Tansy then back again. "But Martha's here with some people from the *Burlington Free Press*."

Ian turned to Tansy, who looked as shocked as he felt. "What's this about?"

Martha moved forward. "Tansy appointed me head of publicity for the festival. Your paintings will definitely be a big attraction." She tipped her head toward the two other people. "They just want to ask you a few questions and take a few shots of you and your paintings."

"Martha," Tansy said pleasantly, looking calm now, "could the three of us have a few minutes together first?"

"Coffee," Edna said, whirling the press duo around, "in the kitchen."

When the door closed behind them, Tansy said, "Martha, you should have talked to me before you invited reporters to Ian's house."

Martha stiffened. "Excuse me, but when you asked for my help, you said I could do whatever I wanted, and that I should decide what would work best. I think that getting information into the state's biggest newspaper is a great way to draw crowds to the festival."

"You're right," Tansy said, "but not without asking Ian's permission first."

For the second time in the last hour, Ian felt like he was getting in over his head. First, Tansy had invited him to dinner. Now Martha wanted his face plastered in the newspapers.

This was what happened when you let people into your life.

"I don't want to do this," he said flatly. "Tell those two to go home."

"For pity's sake, it's not a big deal," Martha said in a huff. "The reporter will ask you a few questions, and the photographer will take a picture of you with one of your paintings. The reporter also might want to interview Tansy and me. Five minutes, and they'll be out of your life."

Ian turned to Tansy. She seemed chagrined, so sad he wanted to hug her. This was his fault, really. He'd told her to choose the best person to do the publicity and talk him or her into the job. Martha Latham probably *was* the best person for the job. Look what she'd done. Twenty-four, forty-eight hours into it and here she was with reporters.

He sighed. "Okay, bring 'em back."

Tansy looked relieved, which made him feel good about his decision. Martha looked triumphant, which made him regret it. She scurried into the hall and called out, "Okay, we're ready now." And when the newspaper people came down the hall, she added, "He just needed to freshen his makeup."

Ha, ha, ha, the reporter and photographer said, and Ian glowered. He pointed at the reporter. "A short interview." Then he turned to the photographer. "One picture. Me with a painting. No pictures of my studio. Or my house. Or my barn. Or my sheep."

The man shrugged. "Sure. One picture is all we have room for in the paper, anyway."

Ian sighed and felt Tansy's hand on his arm. "I'm sorry, Ian," she said again. "But it won't be so bad."

He glanced down at her, at her pretty face and crazy hair, and knew he was doomed. Yes, it *would* be bad, at least for him. And they both knew it. But he'd do it for Tansy.

"One picture," he reminded Martha, leading the way to his studio. This festival was getting out of hand. First he had to shear a sheep in public, now he had to put his paintings on display for the whole world to see. "One picture and that's all. I *mean* it."

And he still meant it an hour later when Martha and newspaper people left with two pages of notes—and more than a dozen photos.

Chapter Eight

Tansy stared at the butcher case at the grocery store in utter confusion. Dinner for Ian had to be wonderful, something that would distract him from the fiasco with Martha. He'd been so obviously upset by the reporter's intrusion that the very least she could do was to try to make amends. And everybody knew that cooking was the way to a man's stomach—or something like that.

But she had no idea what he'd like. He tore into all of Edna's cooking as if he hadn't eaten in weeks, so it was impossible to tell what his favorite was.

"Hi, Tansy," a lilting voice said.

Tansy was relieved to see Lilah beside her. "Thank goodness you're here."

"I have a houseful of boys. I'm *always* here."

Tansy smiled. "Yes, I guess you are. So maybe you can help me. What does Ian like to eat?"

Lilah's expression was priceless. She looked positively stunned. "Are you asking because you're cooking for him?"

Tansy turned her attention back to the meat counter, hoping Lilah wouldn't notice her faint blush. "Yes. He's been such a good sport about the festival that I asked him to dinner tomorrow night. Now that I've done it—and presented it as an offer he couldn't refuse—it has to be good, or you'll find my body at the bottom of the river, tied to his old computer."

Lilah snickered. "I can believe it. Well, he likes meat loaf."

"Meat loaf? I was thinking about steak au poivre, or—"

"No, meat loaf, mashed potatoes, green beans and apple pie. It's his favorite."

"Sounds like a traditional family dinner. Did the boys have it a lot growing up?" Tansy glanced at Lilah, who suddenly seemed very interested in the boneless chicken breasts.

"Hmm. I'm not sure. But I know he likes it now."

Tansy wanted to ask more questions, but it was obvious that Lilah wasn't going to talk about the brothers' upbringing. What was with the Foster brothers? Why did they never talk nostalgically about their childhoods? And where were their parents? As far as she knew, no one in Serenity Valley had ever met them.

She would have to ask Ian tonight where he grew up. Maybe she could finally learn a little more about this attractive—and secretive—man.

"How's the festival coming along?" Lilah asked.

Tansy brightened. She loved discussing the festival. "So wonderfully it almost scares me. I have plenty of volunteers, and people are really starting to take an interest. I think we'll be able to make more than enough money to paint the building."

"Remember, I can always pitch in if you need help," Lilah said.

Tansy appreciated the gesture, but Lilah had plenty to do already. "Thanks, but you have the foster care facility to take care of. I can handle this."

"True, but let me know if you get backed into a corner. I understand how small problems quickly become big problems. So if you find you need help—" she gave Tansy a meaningful look "—or advice about anything, feel free to call."

Tansy assured her she would, tossed a two-pound package of ground sirloin into her basket and headed off to the produce department to look for potatoes and green beans. Her conversation with Lilah had left her with more unanswered questions. Why was everything in Ian's life such a mystery? Why couldn't Lilah drop a few hints about his childhood so that Tansy could understand him better? Lilah had to know at least something about his parents. They were her in-laws, for heaven's sake.

What was so bad that no one would talk about it?

More important, what could she do to help Ian deal with his past?

"WHAT DO YOU THINK, UNCLE Ian?" Nick asked, stepping back from the easel and looking nervously at him.

Ian crossed the room and studied the painting. For a first effort, it was very good. Nick was a natural at utilizing light and shadow to paint more than just a picture. He'd captured emotion on the canvas.

And it broke Ian's heart. The seven-year-old had obviously suffered a great deal in his life. Like Ian's own paintings, Nick depicted life as cruel and lonely. No pretty houses or smiling suns for this little boy.

"It's very good, buddy," Ian said, patting him on the back. "What's it about?"

Nick shrugged his thin shoulders. "I don't know. It's what I felt like painting."

That bothered Ian. "Were you painting the way you feel now?"

Shaking his head, Nick set his brush down. "No. How I used to feel before I came to stay with Daniel."

That was a relief at least. Even though he was out of his element, Ian knew it was important to have this conversation with Nick. The little boy had closed off his past, had never talked to anyone about it, not even the psychiatrist he visited regularly. Ian couldn't let this chance slip by. Nick needed to get his emotions out in the open and deal with them. Ian, of all people, knew that keeping the bad stuff inside did no good.

"How do you feel now that you're at Daniel's?"

Nick grinned. "It's great. Everyone is really nice, and there's always lots to eat and fun things to do." He looked at his sneakers and added, "Plus they don't get mad when you do something wrong. They still like you. But I can't stay forever."

Ian felt as though a hand had reached inside his chest and squeezed his heart. "Why not?"

Nick shrugged again. "They're having a baby, and then there'll be too many people there. They won't have enough food and stuff."

Ian squatted so his face was level with Nick's. "Daniel and Lilah will always have enough food—and love—for you, Nick. You won't have to leave."

Nick wasn't convinced. "Someone could come for me," he said softly, his voice quavering a little. "It happened to one of the other boys. His mom's cancer went away, so she came and got him."

Ian knew which boy Nick meant. "That was an entirely different situation, Nick. His mom was always going to take him back as soon as she got better. But you—"

"Someone could come back," Nick insisted.

"Who would come for you?" Ian asked gently. The same people who'd left Nick alone, lost and hurt, on a rainy night? Over his dead body they would.

"I don't know." Nick's shoulders drooped. "Somebody."

Pain from his own childhood and anger over Nick's tore through Ian. He reached out and hugged the boy. "Trust me. I won't let anybody take you away unless you want to go with them."

"Promise?"

"I promise." Ian had never meant anything more in his entire life.

Then he turned his attention back to Nick's painting. It was dark and sad and lonely. He glanced across the room to the landscape he was working on. It, too, was dark and sad and lonely.

"Hey, buddy, how about both of us try to paint something funny? We can see which of us does the best job, okay?"

The mood lifted, and Nick nodded. "Okay. I can paint funny things, too."

Once Nick was happily painting again—this time using yellow and bright blue—Ian walked across the room and picked up a blank canvas. Something funny. Up until a few weeks ago, he would've had trouble thinking of something funny to paint. His life had been like his landscapes. But a crazy redheaded accountant wouldn't leave him in peace. The past few weeks had been nonstop craziness. His peaceful farm had been overtaken by visitors and his studio now drew more foot traffic than some amusement parks.

Yep, thanks to Tansy, he could think of funny things to paint—starting with a picture of a man shearing a sheep in front of a cotton-candy-eating crowd.

TANSY GLANCED AROUND her small apartment and fretted. Did it look okay? Would Ian like it? His house was so beautiful that she worried he'd find it shabby.

She fluffed a throw pillow, tried to sit, then stood and paced the living room. After a couple of minutes listening to the clock in the corner tick away the seconds, she sat abruptly on one of the dining room chairs.

What was wrong with her? She was a grown woman, the survivor of several—okay, a few—relationships. She wasn't a teenager, so why was she acting like one? Ian was coming to dinner. So what? They'd eat, talk, get to know one another, and maybe do a little more….

Tansy stood and started pacing again. The crisp knock on her front door startled her so much that she let out a little yelp. She needed to calm down. At this rate, she'd self-destruct before they reached dessert.

Taking a deep breath, Tansy opened the front door, and then immediately forgot how to breathe at all. Ian looked so handsome that she couldn't think of anything except how much she wanted to make love with him.

Under a wool overcoat he wore a navy sport coat, a light blue oxford-cloth shirt, a navy-and-gray-striped tie and gray dress slacks. His thick hair was neatly brushed, and in his hands he held a bouquet of chrysanthemums, orange interspersed with the big, frilly white variety. He looked absolutely gorgeous—and seemed as nervous as she was.

"These are for you," he said, handing her the flowers. "I didn't know if you liked flowers, so if you don't, or if you're allergic to them, we can, um, throw them away."

Tansy started to laugh, but smothered it at the last minute. Ian was trying. He just wasn't any better at this than she was.

"Then it's a really good thing I adore bouquets," she said, leading him into the living room, "because it would be a shame to throw this one away."

She lightly touched the blooms. "They're lovely. Where did you find them?"

He fiddled with the collar of his shirt. "In the greenhouse behind the barn. I guess I never got around to showing it to you. Edna grows herbs and vegetables in there." He glanced away from her. "And I grow a few flowers."

If he'd told her that he was able to perform magic she couldn't have been more surprised. Ian was definitely a man of surprises. She'd actually noticed the greenhouse, but Edna had said she used it to grow vegetables during the winter months. She hadn't said a thing about Ian growing flowers.

Tansy tipped her head and drew in the rich, sharp scent of the mums. "I love them," she told him, knowing there was a fairly good chance she was falling a little in love with him, as well.

Rather than look away, Ian held her gaze. The air in the room seemed to crackle with awareness. "I'm glad," he said, his deep voice husky.

Tansy wasn't sure what she would have done if the timer on the oven hadn't started to buzz. She tore her eyes away from Ian, bustled to the kitchen and put the flowers in a vase. After washing her hands, she turned her attention back to dinner. When she glanced toward the doorway, she found Ian standing there, watching her.

"It's meat loaf." Rather than pretend to be psychic, she admitted, "Lilah told me it was a favorite of yours."

"It sure is," he confirmed. "How can I help?"

"You don't have to help," she told him. "Why don't you wait in the living room? I'll call you when it's ready."

"And risk having Edna mad at me? No way. I'm helping, as long as I can take off this tie."

Tansy laughed. "Okay. Deal."

She drained the potatoes, then watched Ian take off his tie. He unbuttoned the top button of his shirt and smiled at her.

"Now I'm all yours. Use me any way you want," he said.

Talk about a poor choice of words. All sorts of devilish ideas popped into her head but she quickly stomped them down.

"I'm not sure what you can do," she said.

Ian nodded toward the pan of steaming potatoes. "Why don't I mash those? Edna showed me how to make mashed potatoes years ago. Squashing things seems to be a skill of mine."

Tansy laughed and agreed. "Sure. Go ahead."

For the next few minutes, they worked in silence. Tansy was surprised how comfortable it was having Ian in her kitchen. It felt...right.

Once they'd set everything on the table, they both dug in. His mashed potatoes were heavenly. "You're right. These potatoes are wonderful."

Ian nodded. "The trick is a lot of cholesterol. Cream, butter, more cream, more butter—Edna says fix them right or don't fix them at all."

"How long have Edna and Joe worked for you?" she asked, wanting to know everything about this man.

"About ten years. Joe started to work for me as a hand, then after the accident, I hired Edna, too."

Tansy was so sad for the couple. "Edna told me about the car accident. She said a drunk driver hit them."

A shadow crossed his face. "Yeah. Joe had only worked for me for a few weeks, and he and Edna were both in the hospital for months. Edna lost her job, so I hired her as soon as she could walk again. Glad I did. I would have starved to death by now."

Tansy leaned forward. "You're such a special man," she said.

Ian met her gaze, then shook his head. "I'm not doing anything special, Tansy. Joe and Edna earn every cent I pay them. They keep the ranch running. I'm the lucky one."

She was glad he felt that way. Since getting to know Edna and Joe, she realized that they were, indeed, almost like parents to Ian. Like his parents? Or like the parents he'd never had?

"How did you meet Tim?" she asked.

"Tim and I have known each other for a few years. He was having trouble getting a job. I hired him because he's great at what he does."

"You also learned sign language," she pointed out.

"No, I already knew that."

"Really? Why?"

"There was a kid in school who taught me some. I learned more on my own."

Interesting. Tansy tipped her head to one side. "You didn't grow up in the valley, I know. Where did you go to school?"

"No. I didn't grow up here." After a few seconds, he added, "I moved around a lot when I was a kid." Before she could say anything, he looked at her. "Enough about me. What about your life?"

He was deliberately changing the subject, just as Lilah had at the grocery store when Tansy had started asking about Ian's past. What was it that made everyone close down when she asked a few questions?

"Everyone knows about me," she said. "My whole family, with the exception of my mother, is involved in politics. In fact, the Appletrees have been a fixture in state politics for generations. We're a loud, head-strong lot, so it would be hard not to know the Appletree saga."

"Did you ever consider *not* going into politics?"

Tansy pretended to be shocked. "An Appletree not in politics? Can't happen."

"Sorry. My mistake," he said with mock humility. "What was I thinking?"

She smiled at him, knowing that for him, those gruff words were his version of raucous hilarity. "That's okay. I'll forgive you this once."

They finished eating, then cleaned up. Ian insisted on helping, and since Tansy's apartment didn't have a dishwasher, she let him wash and she dried. After they finished the last dish, they headed into the living room.

"Dinner was great," Ian said. His height and his broad shoulders made the compact room seem even smaller.

Tansy wanted to ask him to have a seat, she wanted to ask him to stay longer, but she couldn't seem to get her brain to cooperate. All she could think about was pressing her mouth against his and putting her arms around him.

So, being a headstrong Appletree, she walked over to him, stood on tiptoe, and did just that.

IAN HAD BEEN THINKING about making love with Tansy since he'd arrived at her apartment. Actually, he'd been thinking about it before then. In fact, since meeting her, he'd spent pretty much all of his time thinking about ravishing her.

He leaned down and returned her kiss, then shifted them slightly until they sat on the sofa. Once settled, he started to draw Tansy closer, but as usual, she beat him to it. She scooted until she was sitting on his lap, facing him. Somehow she managed to do this without breaking the kiss.

Tansy Appletree was one talented lady.

Ian wrapped his arms around her and deepened the kiss, sliding his tongue inside her mouth to meet hers. Tansy murmured a little sound that he took for approval since she pressed herself closer to him. She wove her fingers through his hair, holding him to her as though she'd never let him go.

He had no idea how long they kissed, but finally, he couldn't take any more. He let her go and leaned his forehead against hers.

"I'm sorry. This is getting out of hand."

His breathing was ragged, as was hers. She nodded. "Yes, it is." She slid off his lap and took his hand. "Come on. Let's move to the bedroom."

It was the last thing Ian had expected her to say. "Are you sure?"

Tansy's smile convinced him she was completely sure. It was all the invitation he needed. He stood and took her hand, following her through the narrow hallway to the bedroom in the back. Once there, he wanted to tell her how beautiful she was, how desirable, but he couldn't come up with the words.

Thankfully, Tansy didn't seem to want to talk. She started kissing him again, and soon they were on the bed, their fingers fumbling with each other's clothes. He kissed and caressed her carefully, slowly, wanting her to know she was special, that she meant a lot to him. He'd never been a man who was good with words, but he was good with his hands, so he showed Tansy exactly how he felt about her.

When they both were frantic with need, he took the condom she offered him, then joined them swiftly. Their lovemaking was intense and powerful, and when it was over, Ian realized that something remarkable had happened here tonight. For the first time in his life, he hadn't just had sex, he'd made love. It was a powerful feeling, one he liked.

He gathered Tansy close, covered them with the blanket they'd kicked to the floor in their passion, then fell asleep.

TANSY COULDN'T HELP HUMMING the next morning while she padded out to the kitchen to start the coffee brewing. Ian was in the shower—*her* shower in *her* apartment—and it felt wonderful. Last night—and this morning—had been amazing. She had never felt so alive, so cherished, in her life.

It was all thanks to Ian.

She made her way to the front door and gathered the Sunday paper off the stoop. On Sundays, she had the Burlington paper delivered so she could keep up on statewide news. One glance at the front page, and she froze. Splashed across the top was a teaser for the lead story in the Life section. It showed a picture of Ian standing next to one of his paintings with the caption, "Local farmer unveils hidden talent."

Tansy's stomach dropped. Oh, no. The reporters had promised Ian it would be a small story. She flipped to the Life section, already knowing what she would find. The article took up a full page and included numerous photos of Ian, his house, his farm—even his sheep. The photographer had taken shots of everything, including his paintings.

Feeling ill, Tansy sank onto the sofa and read the article. In addition to information about Ian and his paintings, it contained quotes from people in town saying what a recluse he was, and how most people didn't know him at all. Then there was the statement from her saying how much the town appreciated Ian's help. Next was Martha saying that Ian had never had much time for anyone before Tansy had encouraged him to participate in the festival. They'd even posted a picture of the foster care facility being built on his land.

It was a wonderful article, very complimentary, very thorough. Most people would be thrilled with it. Ian came across as a rare, extraordinary man.

But it was the type of story a man who valued privacy—a man like Ian—would hate.

She shoved the entire paper under the sofa. She'd show him the article sooner or later, but not now.

Chapter Nine

"My life is a disaster," Ian said the second Daniel opened the door of his veterinary clinic. "I can't believe what's happened."

And he couldn't. This morning, everything had been perfect. A night of love, a huge breakfast to stoke their energies for more love—and then Tansy had shown him the newspaper article.

He could tell she hadn't wanted to. She'd been anxious, as if she already knew what his reaction to it would be. But she hadn't wanted him to hear about it from anybody else, hadn't wanted him to be surprised by a comment from one of the villagers.

He appreciated that, because the article had upset him enough to trigger a hasty retreat—the last thing he'd wanted to do just a few minutes earlier. He'd driven around for an hour before being drawn like a homing pigeon to Daniel's house.

Not to his house, exactly, but to the front stoop of his clinic, which opened into the house. Ian realized gloomily that he'd even parked down the street instead of in the drive, like a cagey thief. He knew Daniel checked on things at the clinic, even on Sundays, and Ian was on the front stoop waiting for him. As soon as he saw the light go on in his brother's office, he hammered on the door.

"How long have you been sitting here?" Daniel asked as he let Ian in.

"An hour. Maybe two." Ian followed him to his office. "I needed some time to think."

"Two hours?" Daniel shook his head. "What were you thinking about? And why didn't you just come into the house? We've been back from church for hours."

"I told you. I needed to think." Ian flopped into the chair facing Daniel's desk. "My life is ruined."

Daniel sat in his desk chair gazing at him with the patient look on his face that both of his brothers knew so well. Daniel was the practical one, which was why Ian needed to talk to him. If anyone could figure out a solution to this mess, it would be Daniel.

"So?" Ian prompted when Daniel didn't offer any advice.

"You haven't told me what's wrong," Daniel pointed out.

Yeah. Right. He hadn't. Ian tossed the Life section of the paper on Daniel's desk. "That's what's wrong. I've had two calls on my cell phone already this morning from agents who want to 'represent my work' and another newspaper has called for an interview."

"I bet it's not that bad," Daniel said as he picked up the paper and started to read.

Not that bad? It was awful. When Tansy had shown him the paper, Ian had realized that everything he and his brothers had worked so hard for all these years might be lost. Although he'd moved to Vermont as an adult, someone from his past might recognize him. And if they did, they might call the newspaper themselves to give them the scoop. Having a criminal record, even as a juvenile, wouldn't win him any friends in this town.

But that hadn't been his first fear. What had worried him most was what Tansy would think if she learned that he'd been arrested for shoplifting, housebreaking, you name it, as a kid, just trying to support himself after his mother abandoned him. Even worse, what would she think if she found out that his brothers weren't actually his biological brothers?

Would she hate him for lying to her? For lying to everyone in the valley?

So he'd panicked when he read the article and had done what he'd assured her he wouldn't do anymore—he ran. Now he was worried that she thought he was a jerk to desert her after spending the night with her.

He ran his hands through his hair. "See? It is bad."

Daniel raised one hand and continued to read. "I haven't finished the article yet."

"Read faster." Ian stood and paced the small office. Finally, Daniel lowered the paper and shrugged.

"It's all good, Ian. Everything in the article is positive."

"But what if somebody recognizes me from the pictures?"

"I doubt that anyone will. The pictures aren't that great, especially the ones of you."

Ian peered at the photos. The ones of his paintings were very clear, but Daniel was right. The few shots of him weren't very good.

"But they still look like me," he moaned.

Daniel shrugged. "If it happens, it happens. We were kids, Ian. We got some bad breaks, made some mistakes, we paid for them, and now it's over. I thought my life would fall apart when Lilah learned the truth, but it didn't. Mike thought Allie would leave him once she learned about his background, but she didn't. Both women understood. Just like Tansy will."

Ian shook his head. "You're wrong about Tansy. It's not like that between us."

Daniel chuckled. "Tell that to someone who might believe it. There's obviously *something* between the two of you. Everyone in town can see it."

"That's not true." But Ian wondered if it was. When would the townspeople have seen them together? Martha had seen them the other day when she brought those blasted reporters, but other than that…of course, in Holman, that was enough. Martha wouldn't need to gossip. Just the question, "Do you know if Tansy and Ian are seeing each other or just working together?" would get the gossip going.

"Where is Tansy now?" Daniel asked. "You should talk it over with her."

"Why?" Ian shook his head. "I'm the one who has to figure out what to do."

"No, what you *need* to do is talk to Tansy."

At Daniel's sharp tone, Ian looked at him. "I don't—"

"Look at the way you're dressed. You obviously went out with her last night and you're wearing the same clothes this morning. I can put two and two together, Ian. You need to find Tansy, tell her you're sorry you ditched her and explain that you were rattled by the article. But now you're fine, and you want to spend the rest of the day with her. Tansy deserves better."

Ian opened his mouth, and then slammed it shut when he realized his brother was right. Tansy did deserve better.

"Fine. Have it your way." Ian headed toward the door. "And for the record, this talk didn't help me one damn bit."

Daniel laughed. "I never said it would."

TANSY HAD TRIED TO BE as low-key as possible when she showed Ian the article, but he'd turned on his heel and fled. He'd overreacted, of course, but publicity was the sort of thing Ian would overreact to.

The way he'd stared at her, then simply stalked out showed that he blamed her for the article. Maybe she deserved the blame. Feeling glum, she decided to bake an old-fashioned coconut cake and was in the middle of frosting it when there was a knock on the front door. She had no idea who it was, but she couldn't help wishing Ian would come back and tell her he really wasn't sorry he'd ever met her.

When she opened the front door, there he was, looking tired, contrite and oh so sexy.

"I'm sorry. I kind of freaked out when I saw that article," he said. "I'm not used to…attention."

Tansy's heart broke for him. She waved him inside and then wrapped her arms around him. "It's okay. I feel responsible for the article, and I know it wasn't what we'd agreed on. I'm so sorry they did that to you. But it's not a bad thing, Ian. Your paintings are wonderful. It's good that you're getting the recognition you deserve."

Ian hugged her for a moment, then stepped back. "That's the thing, Tansy. I don't want to be recognized. I like my simple, quiet life. I don't want people talking about me and looking at my paintings. I want to be left alone."

For a people person like Tansy who had spent her life surrounded by politicians, wanting to be alone was a foreign concept. But she could see how upset Ian was, so she said, "Then that's what we'll try to do. I'll run interference and see if we can get the whole situation to calm down."

"How, Tansy? Agents are calling me. Other papers are calling."

"And tomorrow morning this article will line the bottoms of bird cages," Tansy pointed out. "It will blow over. People will forget. Sure, it may help attract some visitors to the festival, but once that's over, everyone will go back to leaving you alone."

Ian blew out a breath and stared at his shoes. She knew he was trying to decide what to do. She was also half-afraid he was considering telling her he wouldn't be part of the festival. That would be a tragedy. It certainly wouldn't be good for the town because she knew Ian's paintings were going to be a big draw.

But it also wouldn't be good for Ian. As much as he talked about wanting to be alone, he didn't really mean it. He wanted his brothers and their families in his life. He also wanted Joe, Edna and Tim surrounding him. She couldn't help hoping he might also want *her* in his life.

"Give it a couple of weeks," she said. "Let's see what happens. I bet you'll be surprised at how quickly people forget all about you. Before you know it, they'll be scratching their heads and saying, 'Ian who?'"

"I hope so." He gave her a long, considering look. Then he smiled a little, just a small smile that made her heartbeat do a tiny skip. "Well, maybe I don't want *everybody* to forget about me."

Relief seeped through Tansy. She moved into a position directly in front of him. "My, my, Mr. Foster, are you flirting with me?"

"Why yes, Ms. Appletree, I believe I am. Is it working?"

Tansy stood on her tiptoes and brushed his lips lightly with her own. "Hmm. Oh, yeah. Beautifully."

IAN WAS PLEASED TO DISCOVER that Tansy had been right. For the most part, his life settled down over the next week. He and Tansy spent their days finalizing the documentation for the audit. He had a few phone calls from pesky agents and other newspapers, but he turned them all down. At last, they stopped calling.

What didn't change was the way he felt about Tansy. The more time he spent with her, the more time he *wanted* to spend with her. But he had responsibilities and so did she, so after their glorious weekend, they had to be content with kisses and caresses in his office. As soon as the weekend rolled around again, making love with her was all he could think about.

"Do you think Edna and Joe suspect anything?" Tansy asked Sunday morning as they were curled up on her sofa reading the paper.

Last night he'd arrived intending to cook dinner for her, but it hadn't happened. He'd barely made it through the door when he took a good look at her, dropped his grocery bags on the floor and raced her to the bedroom. Dinner was a frozen pizza they baked and took back to bed. He'd never had a better meal.

"Probably. They aren't blind. They know when I don't come home. Edna keeps giving me sappy smiles, so I think she's figured out what's going on."

She glanced at him over the top of the State Government section. "Does that bother you?"

A few weeks ago, it would have. He'd have been enraged at the thought of anybody nosing around in his business, even Edna. But these days, he didn't seem to get upset as often. He wondered what had mellowed him out.

But he really didn't have to wonder. The reason was sitting right in front of him, irresistible in a pair of silky, leopard-print pajamas, which she wore with fuzzy slippers shaped like floppy-eared rabbits, making the foot part of her look about six years old, in dramatic contrast to the rest of her.

He shrugged. "Doesn't bother me much."

"Good. Because I like our Saturday-night routine," she said.

He gazed at her. Did two Saturday nights spent together make a routine? He hoped so.

"I like our routine, too," he said.

Tansy rewarded him with a smile. "I'm glad." Her smile shone on him. "Thank goodness I had that pizza in the freezer. What would you like me to have in the freezer next Saturday night?"

"Anything, as long as it isn't you."

She snickered, then for a few minutes, they read

in silence, which was broken by the ringing of the phone.

"Mom! Hi!" Tansy straightened up on the sofa, slid away from Ian and buttoned one more button of her pajamas.

Amused, Ian meandered into the kitchen to give her some privacy, but he could still hear her, so he went to the bedroom, where he had to face the fact that the apartment was too small for privacy. Back in the living room, in a chair across from the sofa, he inferred without much difficulty that Tansy was trying to talk her way out of going to lunch with her parents.

"It'll be so crowded," she was saying. "Everybody goes there after church. Well, yes, we could call Mike... it's not fair, really, when he makes a point of not taking reservations...you're right, for a state senator he might make an exception...

"All right," she finally conceded, rolling her eyes at Ian. "N-no," she said. "I'll call him. No, really, Mom, it would be better if I did. Okay. Twelve-thirty. Okay. Okay. *Okay*." And at last she hung up. "I have to go to lunch with my parents," she said to Ian. "They're the only people I can't out-persuade."

He nodded. "Sure. I should get back to the farm, anyway. There's a lot I need to do."

Tansy shook her head. "You don't understand. They want you to come, too."

Ian froze. "Your parents know I stayed here last night?"

"Oh, no," Tansy said. "At least, I hope not. They asked because they've heard we've been seeing each other. They'd like to meet you. I was just telling her I'd call you. I could just see her phoning your house, getting Edna, hearing Edna say, 'No, he's not here, he spent the night out.'"

Ian paled. Daniel had told him everybody in town was talking about the two of them, and apparently he'd been right. That blasted Martha Latham. She looked Puritan proper, but did she actually have the sensitivity to sense the electricity shooting between them?

Ian looked at Tansy. She seemed nervous. "Are you uncomfortable because you're afraid I'll say no or that I'll say yes?"

Tansy blinked. "Why would I be upset if you said yes? That would be great."

Ian appreciated her vote of confidence, but it was misplaced. Even the thought of going to lunch with her parents made him nervous. "I'm not exactly good with people, Tansy. Your parents may not like me."

"You don't give yourself enough credit," she said.

He shook his head. "No, you give me too much credit. I'm terrible with small talk, and I don't want to discuss my life or my paintings."

Rather than brush off his concerns, Tansy studied him for a moment. Finally, she said, "They want to meet us at Mike's Diner. There'll be lots of other people around to distract them—"

"Lots of other people to wonder why you've taken me to meet your parents," Ian moaned.

"No, no, my father is notorious for pinpointing people in the valley who'd contribute to his election campaign committee if they saw the light. If worse comes to worst, you can claim a sick sheep and Mike will hide you in the kitchen. And besides," she admitted, "neutral territory will give you an advantage."

Ian didn't want to have lunch with the Appletrees like he didn't want thirty-below-zero temperatures at the farm. But he could tell it meant a lot to Tansy, and since making her happy meant a lot to him, he said, "I couldn't think of anything I'd like to do more than have lunch with your parents."

Tansy rolled her eyes again, appreciating his blatant insincerity. He loved it when she did that. Her eyes were so big, so green. He stopped himself from analyzing the various shades of green and choosing the right one to describe Tansy's eyes.

"But let me be the one to call Mike," Ian said. "I don't want to see any surprise on his face. Or worse."

Tansy's smile was so bright that it made Ian glad he'd agreed. "Deal. And thanks."

"Don't thank me yet," Ian said. "We're looking at a potential disaster here. So remind me again—your father is what? A Democrat? A Republican? Libertarian? Uncommitted?"

TANSY FIDGETED THE ENTIRE WAY to Mike's Diner. As much as she hated to admit it, Ian could have a point. This lunch could very well be a disaster. Although she loved her parents dearly, they could be pushy. They loved to know everything about everyone. They also loved to make suggestions about how one should live.

Neither of those traits would endear them to Ian. Truthfully, this was much too soon for a "meet the parents" meal. She couldn't believe that her parents had asked, especially her mother. The one thing she'd always been able to count on from her mother was common sense.

But her mother had been adamant. And then her father had gotten on the phone and been even more adamant. They were delighted Tansy was seeing someone—although they were piqued by having apparently been the last in town to know it. They simply *had* to meet this exceptional man.

She glanced at Ian. His hands were gripping the steering wheel so tightly she expected it to snap off the column at any second. He'd agreed to this lunch, but she knew he'd rather walk the plank than get to know her parents. She worried this meeting would scare him off. What they had together was too new, too precious to let it be spoiled by interfering parents.

The parking spaces near the diner were full, indicating a big crowd. When Ian had parked around the corner, he turned to her. "Ready?"

Tansy unbuckled her seat belt, then looked at him. "What about you?"

"Ready for it to be over." His tone was grim.

She sighed. "Promise this won't change what we have," she whispered.

"Why should it?"

"It won't, not if we don't let it. I know you hate this, but they mean well. They're my parents. We only have to be nice for an hour tops, and then we can go back to my apartment."

Ian leaned over and gave her a gentle, lingering kiss. "I promise it won't ruin anything. I'll be on my best behavior."

Tansy realized it wasn't his behavior she was worried about. "You're a wonderful man, Ian Foster," she said.

"Make sure you tell your parents that," he countered.

They climbed out of the car and raced to the diner to escape the cold. As she'd predicted, Mike's was overflowing with the customers who ate out after church.

"Hi, Tansy. Ian," Mike said, weaving around the tables to join them by the front door. "Good thing you called ahead. I set aside one of the tables in the back so you can talk."

Ian frowned at his brother. "I don't want to be in the back. It's too quiet. We want to be out front."

Tansy nodded. "Yes, please, Mike. We're both a little nervous about this lunch with my parents. Limiting the conversation would be a good thing." Plus the fact that her father might get involved in conversation with constituents who dropped by the table to say hello.

Mike opened his mouth, looked from her to Ian, and finally shrugged. "A noisy table near the front it is," he said, waving at one of the waitresses. "At Mike's Diner, we aim to please."

Within a couple of minutes the place settings had been removed from the table in a cozy alcove against the rear wall of the restaurant and moved to a central table near the window. Ian held Tansy's chair for her as she sat. She glanced around, noting the boisterous families and chatting friends surrounding them. And staring at them. Where the heck were her parents?

The volume was at a pleasant, white noise sort of level when at last they stepped in. Since Roger Appletree was the state senator for Serenity Valley, he was instantly surrounded by people who wanted to shake his hand, just as Tansy had hoped. Priscilla was also a valley favorite. She stopped and chatted with several people after first waving at Tansy.

Tansy saw Ian take a deep breath and realized she was holding hers. She forced herself to exhale.

"It'll be fine," she told Ian, then scooted her chair closer to his.

Ian stood and held out his hand as her parents reached the table. "Hello, Mrs. Appletree. Senator."

Tansy's father shook Ian's hand. "It's Roger and Priscilla," he said. He dropped a kiss on Tansy's cheek and would have held the chair for Priscilla, but Ian beat him to it.

Her father winked at Tansy and took his seat. "So nice of you both to join us. Your mother and I love getting out on a Sunday afternoon."

"Mike's Diner is my favorite restaurant. Absolute favorite," Priscilla said, smiling at her daughter and Ian. "I don't just mean in the valley—I mean anywhere in the world. The food is lovely, and the people are wonderful."

"Mike tries to do it right," Ian said.

"I sure do." This came from Mike, who had walked up while they were talking. He grinned at the group and handed out menus. "Sorry I couldn't get you a quieter table in the back. I wanted to, but it's the funniest thing, they were all taken." His eyes twinkled at Tansy.

Roger shrugged. "Nothing wrong with this table. Right in the middle of things. That's where I like to be."

"How are the wedding plans coming along?" Tansy asked Mike.

"Great." Mike beamed. "I just want it to be over. I mean the wedding. I can't wait to get married. Did I mention yet how much I love my fiancée? I'm the luckiest man on the earth. Love really changes your life."

"True, true," Roger said. "Nothing like it."

"That's right. There's nothing like finding that one special woman." With that, Mike slapped Ian on the back and headed back to the kitchen. Tansy shot a worried look at Ian, but he seemed calm, despite what his brother had just done.

"So, Ian, I understand you paint," Priscilla said, smoothly covering, as usual, any potential awkwardness.

"I do," Ian said.

"I saw the photos in the paper. You're quite talented. Have you considered having a show?" Priscilla tapped Roger on the arm. "Bunny Piedmont owns a gallery in New York, doesn't she? We could talk to her on your behalf."

"Don't let the name fool you," Roger said. "Bunny's a sharp businesswoman. She'd treat you right and give you a great start. I'll give her a call in the morning and ask if she has any open time in the next few months."

Tansy jumped in. "Enough, Mom and Dad. Leave Ian alone. He appreciates your help, but he doesn't want to go any farther than manning a booth at the festival just yet."

Ian thanked her with his eyes. "Yes. I appreciate it, but I'd rather not."

"But why not? You could—" Her mother fell silent when she caught the look Tansy sent her.

"How've you been, Dad?" Tansy asked, deliberately

changing the subject. "I haven't had a good talk with you in ages."

"Fine, fine. Busy as always. Did you read that article in this week's *Valley News* about Telman Industries wanting to develop the property between Holman and LaRocque? Not going to happen. It would ruin the ecosystem. They'll have to come up with a new plan."

Happy to have latched on to a neutral topic, Tansy engaged her father in a debate about zoning ordinances and proposed changes to the state park system. She made certain to pull Ian and her mother into the conversation, as well. While they ate, she continued to direct the verbal traffic, which enabled her to stop her parents from cross-examining Ian.

When things got repetitive, she brought up the festival. Avoiding any reference to Ian's paintings, Tansy outlined the schedule of events. "Ian has agreed to organize a 'sheep to sweater' booth, which will be fun."

"I heard about that," Priscilla said, "and think it will be a fascinating display. Not just for the kids," she added. "I'll learn a lot myself."

"It was Tansy's idea," Ian volunteered.

"And a great idea," her father said, patting her hand. "A politician has to come up with innovative ideas to help the citizens of her town—or her state. Tansy's a natural at it. That's why she has a great political career ahead of her."

"I don't know yet, Dad. I'm happy being mayor and running my accounting practice."

"You're happy at the moment. But there's so much more you could do, and so much more you have to offer the world." Her father frowned at her. "Why the sudden change of heart?"

"I haven't had a change of heart. I never said I aspired to be more than a really good mayor," she said. Knowing this conversation had the potential to veer off in an uncomfortable direction, she ended with, "I'm still mulling over my future."

"Futures don't just happen," Roger said. "You create them. You have to set goals and fix your sights on them. The valley is a nice place, but you don't want to hide here your whole life."

He was so careful not to look at Ian, when ordinary good manners would have driven him to include the whole table in his gaze, that Tansy knew what he was thinking. He thought Ian was hiding from the world, not taking advantage of the opportunities his artistic talent offered him. Moreover, he was making it painfully clear that he didn't want his daughter doing the same thing.

It was amazing what her father could say with only a look and a few words.

Tansy drew in a deep breath and was about to tell him that being happy was what life was truly about, but she was spared when the waitress appeared to tell them there was no bill since the lunch was on Mike. With a lot of hand-shaking and forced smiles, they all stood and gathered their coats. Her mother promised to call her the next day, and her father gave her a big bear hug.

On the way to the car, Tansy nervously looked at Ian. "I'm sorry Dad said what he did. I don't agree with him."

His expression was thoughtful, which upset Tansy more. "They only want what's best for you."

"So do I. And what's best for me is *you*." Tansy took his hand, threaded her fingers through his and smiled at him. "Now let's go back to my apartment so you can show me just *how* good you can be for me."

Chapter Ten

For a winter Saturday morning, it was a nice one. On the small pond near Ian's house, Daniel and his boys were trying to ice skate, but in Daniel's case, it wasn't skating, it was a manly struggle to stay upright.

This family gathering was just what Ian needed. In the week since the unnerving lunch with her parents, Tansy had finished loading all the necessary software onto the new computer and had given him basic instructions on how to use it—with delicious promises to help anytime he got stuck, which he planned to do as often as possible.

Ian's education had been her "overtime project." She'd already transformed his handwritten spreadsheets into a computerized thing of beauty, had checked every receipt with his entries—no errors on his part, he thought smugly—and had assured him they were ready for the audit.

The downside was that since she'd finished, Tansy had spent most of her time in her own office dealing with other clients and, of course, the festival. Although he still saw her every day, Ian was surprised by how much he missed her. He liked having her around the house.

It had been a long wait for their weekend together, but when Daniel called and asked to bring the boys skating, Ian couldn't refuse, so he invited Tansy, too. Later this evening, he'd have her all to himself.

He could hardly wait.

"I think his career as a professional figure skater may be limited," Ian said when Daniel wobbled again and almost fell. "Be careful out there, old man."

Daniel just laughed and kept on skating.

Daniel's wife, Lilah, said, "But he definitely gets good-sport points. He's doing it for the boys."

Family meant the world to Daniel, and that included his foster boys. There wasn't anything the man wouldn't do for them, and they all knew it.

"He's such a special person," Tansy said, coming over to stand next to Ian. "Do you skate?"

"No. Never learned. Don't want to now." He looked at her. She was wearing a bright blue parka that made her even prettier than usual. For a moment, he just drank in the sight of her, then he smiled slowly. These past few weeks together had been some of the best of his life. Truthfully, they had been the *very* best of his life.

"Ahem," Lilah said loudly. "I think I'll sit down for a minute."

Lilah's comment snapped them both out of the spell that surrounded them.

"Are you okay?" Ian asked his pregnant sister-in-law. "Is it too cold out here for you?"

"I'm fine. I'll just rest a while on the bench," Lilah said airily, but the smile she flashed Ian was mischievous.

After Lilah had settled on the wooden bench, Ian turned his attention back to Tansy, whose face was quite a bit pinker than it had been. "Do you skate?"

"I have, but I outgrew my skates."

He glanced down at her tiny feet and arched his eyebrows at her.

"I had my last pair when I was six," she told him. "I simply hated skating. So while everybody else skated…"

"What are you doing?" he asked her when she reached down and gathered up a handful of snow. He took a step back. "You're not going to throw that at me, are you?"

Tansy laughed and knelt, gathering more snow. "You're not very trusting, are you? No, I'm going to build a snowperson."

"Snowperson?"

Tansy tipped her head so she was looking up at him. Her eyes twinkled as she said, "Hey, I'm politically correct."

Ian smiled and watched her work for a moment. "Want some help? I'm pretty good at building snowpeople."

She considered his offer for a moment. "What qualifications do you have, Foster? I've never seen you build one, so how do I know you're any good? I'm an expert snowperson builder. I can't be caught working with amateurs."

Ian pretended to ponder her question. "I've had experience with sculpture. That's all this is, a snow sculpture."

Tansy shook her head. "Doesn't count. Your sculptures could have been horrible. There was some reason you stuck to painting."

"True." He glanced at his brother and the boys. Seeing that Nick had stopped skating and was now sitting on the bench with Lilah, Ian had an idea.

"Hey, buddy. Want to help build a snowperson?"

Nick grinned at him. "Sure."

The boy joined Ian and Tansy, and Ian put an arm around his shoulders. "I brought a reference."

Tansy smiled at Nick. "Oh, good, someone to vouch for your uncle Ian. He tells me he can build snowpeople, but I'm not sure he can."

Nick started amassing snow. "Of course he's good at it. Uncle Ian is good at everything."

Tansy stood and considered Ian. "Hmm. Is that a fact?"

"I seem to remember you telling me the same thing recently." Ian raised one eyebrow, which made Tansy both laugh and blush.

"Um, yes, I think I may have." Without taking her gaze off Ian, she asked Nick, "So do you think we should let Uncle Ian help us?"

Nick nodded so enthusiastically the hood of his parka bobbed up and down. "You bet. Uncle Ian is the *best*."

"I completely agree," Tansy said softly. "Uncle Ian is the best."

Ian smiled at her. In the past few weeks, he'd had so much fun with Tansy. He'd also started to feel…happy. It wasn't an emotion he had a lot of experience with, but he really liked it.

In his opinion, his life had really begun when he'd met Daniel and Mike. Being with them, becoming brothers and forming a family had given him the confidence he needed to succeed. But now they were both establishing their own families with women who loved them.

Ian had started to think he was missing something until Tansy had danced into his life. She was so full of energy and laughter and spark that it made his life seem so much fuller. He woke up each day excited about seeing her. In only a few short weeks, she had changed his world.

Without thinking, he lightly touched her face, then leaned forward and kissed her.

"Uncle Ian!" Nick shrieked. "Tansy is your girl-friend!"

On Monday night, Town Hall was packed. Tansy couldn't have been happier as she watched people continue to stream inside. The festival was this weekend, so they only had a few days for the final preparations. She'd woken up this morning half-afraid that no one would show up for this last meeting, but thankfully, she'd been wrong. One more chance to touch base with the committees, meet and explain the program to the craftspeople. After this, they'd be ready to decorate Town Hall inside and out, set up the booths and help the participants think of ways to display their work. It would be a very busy week, and Ian's audit fell right in the middle of it.

The festival would open Friday evening at six and run through Sunday. Tansy only hoped they could draw in enough people during that time frame, since repainting the old building properly, scraping and priming the peeling clapboard, was an expensive proposition.

She was thrilled by the response from craftspeople. The committee had garnered potters and woodcarvers, jewelry designers and a famous glassblower, not just from Vermont but from New Hampshire and Massachusetts. Most of them had managed to make it here for the meeting, and the rest had promised to show up early on Friday.

But her biggest hope was Ian. Although he was convinced no one was going to buy his paintings, Tansy knew better. People were going to snap them up.

Even though Ian had no interest in a gallery show in New York, he had agreed to let her parents' friend Bunny help price the pieces. Tansy had carefully taken digital photos of each canvas and sent them to Bunny. Although this wasn't the best approach, it was all they could do.

Bunny had been enthusiastic about Ian's work. All last week, she'd tried repeatedly to get Ian to agree to have a show in her gallery, but he kept saying no. Finally Bunny had given up, saying that if she couldn't woo him with fame and fortune, then nothing would make him change his mind. She'd realized that the only reason Ian was participating in the festival was to help his own small town.

Once Bunny had stopped pressuring him about the show, the two of them began to argue enthusiastically about prices. Again, it was Bunny who caved, suggesting sums high enough to reflect the quality of the work but moderate enough that thrifty Vermonters could afford them. Tansy had already set aside two paintings for herself, and her parents, brother and both sisters had earmarked others. Heck, at this rate, Ian really wouldn't have much left to sell to outsiders. The Appletrees were building a monopoly.

Speaking of Ian, he should have been here by now. Tansy stood on tiptoe to scan the crowd milling around the hall. He still hadn't arrived. She could hardly wait to see him. They'd spent Saturday and Sunday together, but she'd only seen him briefly this morning when she'd stopped by the farm to gather up all the papers for the audit. One of his sheep was sick, so he'd been distracted. He'd said hi, given her a quick kiss, and run out of the office to meet Daniel in the barn.

"So where is Ian?" Martha asked loudly as she bustled toward Tansy. "He's a vital part of this festival. If he drops out, many people will be upset."

Tansy took it that one of those people would be Martha herself. "He'll be here. He wants to check over our three-section extravaganza for the sheep demonstration and also see where his paintings will be placed."

Tansy's words obviously did nothing to allay Martha's concerns, since the older woman continued to frown at her. "Tansy, if that man stands us up—"

"You'll what?" A familiar male voice asked from behind Tansy.

Tansy smiled and spun around. She was on the brink of hugging Ian when she caught herself. Oops. That wouldn't do—the whole town would officially know they were involved. Sure, people might suspect at the moment, but they didn't know for certain. If she hugged Ian, they *would*.

"Hi, Ian," she said brightly.

Ian smiled briefly at her and looked back at Martha. "What will you do, Martha?"

Undaunted, Martha moved closer. "You know the town is counting on you, Ian. I was afraid you were about to let us down. This is important. You *owe* this community."

Tansy's hackles went up. "Excuse me, Martha. Ian doesn't owe us anything. He has kindly done everything we've—I've—pushed him to do for us. Don't threaten him."

Martha's frown faded slowly and was replaced by something resembling glee. "I knew it. I knew you two were seeing each other. Karen Montgomery said she couldn't believe it, but I knew. Why else would you have taken him to the diner to meet your parents?"

Tansy was stunned. She was still angry at Martha for her earlier comment, and now she was unsettled by this new turn of events. "Martha, I don't think—"

Martha's eyes were sparkling. "So, is it serious?"

It was now painfully obvious that Martha wanted a gossip scoop. Tansy groaned and turned to Ian. "I'm sorry that..."

Her voice trailed off when she realized he was smiling. At her questioning look, he shrugged. "What else can we expect in Holman?"

"So?" Martha prompted again.

"You've caught us. Tansy and I are dating," Ian said. He gave Tansy a sidelong glance, then focused on the older woman. "Now, we're trusting you to keep it to yourself. We know what an *honorable* woman you are, so I'm sure if you give us your *word* that you won't tell a *soul*, then you won't."

Tansy struggled not to laugh at the earnest expression on Ian's face. He'd apparently taken lessons in manipulation from her. He was playing Martha against herself and laying it on thick. On one hand, the Selectperson did staunchly maintain how trustworthy and honorable she was. She often held herself up as a standard she expected others to match.

On the other hand, she loved to gossip, and news that Tansy and Ian were dating was too juicy to keep to herself. Her friends would eat it up, and Martha would be raised to queen bee status for uncovering the truth.

Watching Martha struggle with her internal conflict was a sight to see. "I, um, I don't really see why it should be a secret," she said. "There's no harm in people knowing."

"But we're asking you, as an honorable woman—and our *close* personal friend—not to tell them," Ian said. "Will you agree?"

A couple of seconds ticked by, then Martha blurted out, "Fine! I won't tell anyone!" She paused again. "What if somebody asks me? May I confirm—"

Ian fixed her with his gaze, moving in a little closer. "If anyone asks you, tell them you have no idea."

As Martha stomped away, Tansy chuckled. "Ian Foster, you are one devious man."

Ian shrugged. "It won't last. Before the evening is over, everyone here will know. I just wanted her to think about what she was doing before she did it."

Tansy glanced around the room. Most people were busy building booths and painting signs, but a few were looking their way. Ian was right. By the end of the evening, she was sure that word would have spread.

Which pleased her no end. She *wanted* people to know. She was proud of Ian. More important, she knew firsthand what a wonderful man he was. It was about time the rest of the town discovered how smart, witty and kind Ian was.

Still, she knew Ian might not be too happy about their relationship becoming public knowledge. She glanced up at him. "It doesn't bother me, but I guess it would bother you."

The old Ian, the man she'd met just a few short weeks ago, would have scowled and ranted about the gossips in this town. But he'd changed since then. Tansy had witnessed his transformation, and this new Ian was much more understanding.

"Actually, it doesn't bother me in the least. I don't care if people know." He glanced around the room, then nodded toward Martha, who was making a beeline for a group of townsfolk. "She's about to spill our secret right now."

Tansy nodded. "I'm afraid she is."

"Are you *positive* you don't mind if people find out?" Ian asked her.

Nothing would make Tansy happier than having the whole town know about them. "Not at all. I welcome it."

"Hey, Martha!" Ian hollered.

Martha, along with everyone else in the room, turned their way.

"Thanks for keeping our secret," Ian said. Before Martha had a chance to spill the beans, Ian gave Tansy a look of pure mischief.

Then he kissed her—in front of the entire town.

And Tansy kissed him back. What else could a woman do?

ON THE DAY OF THE AUDIT, Ian wasn't sure what he expected when Tansy pulled up in front of his house, but it wasn't what he saw. Tansy always dressed nicely, but today she was in full accountant war-gear. Tailored navy suit, matching pumps with moderate heels, tan briefcase, hair pulled back neatly and secured at her nape.

"I'm intimidated just looking at you," he said, taking her briefcase.

Tansy laughed and tapped him on the arm. "You don't look so bad yourself."

"Isn't he a sight?" Edna beamed at him as if she'd never seen him in a suit before. Now that he thought about it, she probably hadn't. "He should dress up more often."

Ian turned to look at his friend and housekeeper. "Yes, the sheep would really appreciate it."

Behind him, he heard Tansy laugh, the sweet sound touching him like a caress. "They might. I know *I* do."

Ian turned to face Tansy. She looked so neat and prim and proper that he wanted to kiss her until she melted.

"Well, in that case..." He leaned down, and ignoring the little laugh from Edna, planted his mouth on Tansy's. It was a token kiss—the melting would have to wait.

In the past few days, he'd stopped worrying about people knowing how much he cared for Tansy. This woman had come to be a very important part of his life, and the other people he cared for might as well know that.

"Hmm, nice," Tansy said. "But don't you want to see how the audit turns out before you kiss me?"

The audit was the last thing on Ian's mind. "It'll be

fine. The return is correct, we have all of the required documentation, and thanks to you, everything is organized and easy to read."

"Breakfast," Edna said, bustling toward the kitchen. "You two can't head off on such an important day without a full stomach."

Although Ian would have preferred to be alone with Tansy, he couldn't disappoint Edna, so he and Tansy followed her to the kitchen. Edna had made a pot of fresh coffee plus scrambled eggs, brown-sugar oatmeal, homemade wholegrain toast, sausage patties and mixed fruit. Tansy and Ian dug in while Edna and Joe headed off to feed the hands.

"She's a wonderful cook," Tansy said. "This is fabulous. I usually don't like oatmeal, but hers is special."

Ian nodded. "She's a special lady. And Joe's a great guy."

"And so are you," Tansy said, holding Ian's gaze. "You really are. I can't tell you what these last few weeks have meant to me. I've never...felt like this before."

For the first time in his life, Ian wished that words came easily to him. He wanted to tell Tansy just how much she meant to him, but he couldn't think of the right way to put it.

So he settled for the truth. "I'm not a guy who can say a lot of fancy things, and I've never been comfortable talking about my feelings."

Tansy patted his right hand. "I know. It's okay."

Ian shook his head and forged on. "But you've made me come alive, Tansy Appletree. It's like I was stuck out in the rain and cold for years, and now you've brought me into the warmth and light."

Tears formed in Tansy's eyes. "Oh, Ian. I feel the same way."

He knew she did. This was something he needed to tell her, something he needed her to hear before the audit or the festival or any of the other things they were doing together. It was important for her to understand that what he felt had nothing to do with gratitude.

"I've never said this to anyone in my life, but I love you," he said slowly, finding the words much easier than he had thought.

The tears in Tansy's eyes overflowed. Ian leaned forward with a napkin and dabbed at them. "Hey, I didn't mean to make you sad."

Tansy shook her head. "I'm not crying because I'm sad, I'm crying because I'm happy."

Ian had never understood "happy tears" because to him it seemed kind of odd, but he was glad that was why she was crying. "That's a relief."

He waited, hoping she would say she loved him back, but she just kept crying and smiling at him. Ian started to get nervous. Maybe she *didn't* love him back. Maybe she liked hanging around with him, but she didn't love him.

Maybe he was an idiot and had misread the signals. Finally he said, "It's okay if you don't feel the same way, I just thought…"

Tansy seemed confused for a moment, then with a little yelp, she jumped into his lap and rained kisses on his face. "Ian, I love you, too. I've thought it so many times over the last few weeks that I guess I assumed I'd said it a million times. I love you, I love you, I love you…" She halted to kiss him deeply.

Ian had been scared, but now he felt as if nothing could ever frighten him again. At the moment, nothing would make him happier than spending the day in bed with Tansy, but he knew they had to get going.

With a self-conscious flurry of activity, Ian and Tansy gathered what they needed for the audit and climbed into his truck. Montpelier was an hour and a half away from Holman. On the way to the IRS office there, as if she was trying to distract them both from thoughts of love, Tansy chattered about the festival and his paintings. Ian surprised himself by joining in. She made him want to talk. She made him believe she cared about his opinions and wanted to hear them.

It was one more reason he loved her.

When they reached the State Street building that housed the IRS offices, they made their way to the waiting room. They weren't alone. Uncomfortable-looking people thumbed through documents, fidgeted and sighed. Ian didn't feel uncomfortable. A lot had happened since he'd opened that letter and panicked. Now they were prepared. Or, Tansy was prepared, and Ian trusted her completely.

When it was finally their turn to meet with the auditor, Ian was calm and collected. Since he'd prepared the original return, he was the one who explained it carefully and quietly, showing the spreadsheets and neatly bound documentation to the auditor. He answered the man's questions and dealt with the concerns that had caused the corporation to be audited in the first place. All the documentation was there and everything added up.

"I told you it would be fine," Tansy said, practically dancing to the sidewalk when they left. "Piece of cake."

"Only because the way you made everything so clear," Ian told her. Her professional demeanor had vanished. Now she reminded him of an elf. He'd wanted to say, "Only because you looked so cute."

He glanced across the street at the gold-domed statehouse. It was rare that he found himself in the capital city, and he wanted to celebrate with Tansy. "How about we treat ourselves to something extraordinary? Something we've never done before."

She linked her arm through his as they walked to the truck. "Like what?"

Ian scanned the territory. They were in the middle of downtown. There were government and office buildings, but also restaurants and small shops. "We'll case the joint first." A few minutes later he nodded toward a restaurant on Main Street. "How about I treat you to the first lunch I've had in years anywhere except Mike's Diner? Well, except for a sandwich I ate when I was still running away from you."

Tansy laughed. "You're on. And I promise not to tell Mike, not about today or the sandwich."

The restaurant was run by the Vermont Culinary Institute, and the food was innovative and delicious, but they both made a point of comparing it unfavorably to Mike's offerings, then rolling their eyes at each other. When they'd finished, Ian said, "Any museums in Montpelier?"

"Yes, in fact," Tansy said, "and it's a little gem. It's been here forever, and by forever I mean since 1896, but along with the historical pieces, they display work by emerging artists, too." She fluttered her lashes at him. "Since you're an emerging artist, you'd probably enjoy it."

Ian loved museums. Loved examining the painting styles of other artists. But thinking about it for a second, he realized he'd better start thinking about somebody other than himself. "Not unless you'll get the same kick out of it that I will."

Tansy looked up at him. The cold had made her cheeks pink, which only enhanced the deep green of her eyes. "I enjoy museums immensely, but no one ever wants to go with me. We took a family trip to New York. Mom wanted to go to plays. Dad was totally fixated on the appointment he had with the mayor. Basil wanted to see the Yankees, especially since they were playing the Red Sox, and my sisters headed straight for Macy's. All alone," she said, putting on a Little Match Girl face, "I went to the Metropolitan Museum, and I got so excited that I was late getting back to the hotel room. My folks were close to calling the police."

"How old were you?"

"Thirteen."

"And they let you go out alone?" Ian was astounded. Her parents seemed to be the overprotective kind, which had made him envious.

Tansy grinned. "After all those years in Vermont, they didn't know any better." Her smile broadened. "And I didn't tell them. Maybe," she said, suddenly sounding shy, "someday we can go to New York or Chicago or Boston and pig out on museums."

He couldn't wait for that "someday, maybe," moment, and not just for the museums.

The one in Montpelier was everything Tansy had said it would be—small, but fascinating. Paintings by the artist for whom the museum was named, and paintings by artists who were clearly on the cutting edge. Ian wandered silently through the rooms, examining brush techniques, painting styles. Tansy stayed by his side, but for once, she was quiet, letting him fall under the spell of the art.

He couldn't tear himself away until some inner signal caused him to glance at his watch. "We'd better start for home," he said, and ushered her out the door.

"I guess so," she said at last, and gave him another one of those smiles that made his heart somersault, "before my parents call out the State Troopers. Actually, in this case it would be Martha calling out the troopers. There's still so much festival business to be taken care of before Friday night."

"I've had a great day," he told her on the way to the car.

"In spite of the audit?"

"I even enjoyed the audit."

"No kidding? Maybe we can get one next year, too."

He growled as he wrapped his arm around her shoulders so tightly he almost lifted her off the street. "You are a devil, Tansy Appletree." *And I love you to distraction.*

When they reached the farm, he said, "Thank you. Thank you for everything. Thank you for saving my reputation with the government—"

Tansy laughed. "I bet you say that to all the CPAs who help you ace an IRS audit."

Ian shook his head and leaned toward her. "No, ma'am. Just you." Then he kissed her, slowly, wishing he had time to do a lot more.

The porch lights flicked on and he pulled away. "Busted," he said. "Remind me to talk to Edna about leaving me alone when I'm kissing you."

"Will do." Tansy unbuckled her seat belt and pushed open her door.

"Want to come in for a minute?" Ian climbed out of the truck and was heading to Tansy's side when the front door of the house opened. Edna and Joe stepped onto the porch, followed by an older woman. Ian glanced at them, called out a hello, then froze. Slowly, he turned his attention back to the group on the porch. Edna was obviously nervous, Joe was frowning, and the older woman was—

"Looks like you have company." Tansy had slipped up beside him. "I have to be going home, anyway."

Ian kept staring at the woman as Tansy gathered her belongings from the truck and waved goodbye to Edna and Joe. He walked her to her car and waited while she got it warmed up.

"I'll see you tomorrow," she said with a bright smile. "Dream about me tonight."

Ian watched her drive away, then looked back at the woman. His heart was racing, and anger tore through him. Every instinct told him to flee to Daniel's house, somewhere safe. He didn't want to talk to her. Didn't want to see her.

But he was too old to run away from his problems, so, reluctantly, he stepped toward the porch. When he reached the steps, he gazed up at the woman, ice running through his veins.

"Hello, Mother," he said.

Chapter Eleven

Ian's heart pounded hard in his chest, and he willed himself to calm down. He could handle this. He wasn't a kid anymore. His mother could no longer hurt him.

"Hello, Ian," she said. She took a step toward him, then stopped. She must have noticed his expression. Ian didn't want her anywhere near him.

Edna and Joe had slipped back inside. Although the last thing he wanted was his mother in his house, they couldn't stand outside in the cold.

He walked around her and held the door. "Let's talk."

His mother passed by him and he showed her into the living room. He hadn't seen her since his teenage years, but she looked almost the same. Older, sure. Her dark hair gray now. A little more haggard. But she'd always been rail-thin and brittle-looking with dark circles under her eyes. Cheryl O'Donnell still looked like a woman on the verge of collapse.

She sat on the edge of the leather couch. Ian took the chair across from her. The tension in the room was almost unbearable, and Ian wanted this meeting over as quickly as possible.

"Why are you here?" Ian asked.

"I saw your picture in the paper, and I just couldn't believe it was my little boy." She smiled slightly, and then waved one hand. "I didn't think it was you at first because your last name was different. But then I realized it was. Why did you change your name?"

"To forget the past. I wanted to start over," he told her flatly.

Again, she gave him a little smile and glanced around the room, seeing, he was afraid, his recent— *very* recent—affluence. "Oh, I see. So, um, how have you been?"

How had he been? How had he been since she abandoned him and left him to fend for himself? What the hell kind of question was that?

"Why are you here?" he asked again through gritted teeth.

Cheryl seemed to age before his eyes. "I've had a tough time, Ian. I know I wasn't the best mother in the world—"

"You weren't a mother at all. I raised myself," he spat at her. "And then you left, and I continued to raise myself. So, Cheryl—" he couldn't bear to call her *mother* "—I'll ask you again—why are you here?"

"Because I want a second chance," she said, anguish in her voice. "Because I want to know my son."

Ian watched tears roll down her face and told himself not to soften. Cheryl was a master manipulator, but unlike Tansy, her intentions were selfish. She manipulated people into feeling sorry for her, and she never accepted responsibility for her actions. She blamed the liquor for her problems, not herself for drinking.

"I don't want to know you," he said flatly. It might be blunt and unfeeling, but it was the truth. He'd worked hard to build a good life for himself. He wouldn't let her destroy that life, especially not now that Tansy was part of it.

Cheryl rubbed her hands across her face. "Look, I know you hate me, and I deserve it. But I want to show you that I've changed."

"It no longer matters. I don't even know you anymore," Ian informed her.

"How can you be so cruel?" she asked. "What made you like this?"

"You did," he scoffed. "You taught me what cruelty is. I can't have you in my life, ever again."

His mother started to speak, then closed her mouth and stared at her hands in her lap. For several long moments, they sat in silence, and she finally raised her head.

"Do you believe people can change, Ian? Look at you. Look how you've changed. I've changed, too. I don't drink anymore. You said you wanted to start over. Well, I want to start over, too. Don't you think people deserve a second chance?"

Ian wanted to tell her no, she didn't deserve a second chance. But he couldn't say the words. His whole life had been about second chances. He'd gotten a second chance when he'd met Daniel and Mike. They'd all gotten a second chance when they'd moved to the valley.

And now he had a second chance with Tansy in his life.

He sucked a deep breath into his lungs and released it slowly. Tansy. He knew what Tansy would tell him to do. She'd want him to give his mother that second chance. So would Daniel and Mike. The people he cared most about would be the first ones to tell him to show kindness. Hatred would get him nowhere. It would only eat at him and destroy his world.

If he turned his mother away now, he wouldn't be the man Tansy deserved. He wouldn't be the brother Daniel and Mike deserved. So for them, he said, "You can stay for a couple of days. But you need to stay on the farm. I don't want you going into town. I have a life here, and you're not going to destroy it."

Cheryl's smile was hesitant, but she did smile. "Thank you, Ian. You won't regret this."

He fixed her with a stern gaze. "You're right. I won't, because you're going to behave. No drinking. You have to promise or you can't stay."

She shook her head. "I won't drink."

He had to tell her one more thing. "You need to know that I didn't just change my name. I have two friends that I met when I was a teenager. We've become brothers by choice. We all changed our last names to Foster, and we take care of each other like real brothers do. Their names are Daniel and Mike."

She didn't seem to find his confession odd. Instead, she said, "That's nice. I'm glad you have people in your life who care about you."

"People around here don't know that we aren't true brothers," he told her. "Not even Edna and Joe, who let you in, or my farmhands. And you can't tell them otherwise."

His mother nodded once again. "Of course. I won't say a word."

Ian studied her for a moment, hoping he wouldn't regret letting her stay. She could destroy his life in so many ways. The risk he was taking was huge.

But he couldn't turn her away.

"I'll have Edna show you the guest room." He glanced into the hallway. "Do you have luggage?"

She shook her head. "No. I'm, um, currently in a somewhat tight financial bind."

Ian felt his muscles tense. Of course she was. So what else was new? "How did you get here?"

"A friend drove me."

Ian knew he should ask more questions, but he couldn't. Not right now. He needed to think. He also needed to talk to Daniel and Mike.

Then he needed to talk to Tansy.

He knew, deep down, that his life was about to change, and not for the better.

TANSY WAS CURIOUS ABOUT the woman who'd been at Ian's house, but she didn't want to pry. She knew Ian would tell her about his guest if it was important, which apparently it was. Just before midnight, he called and said he was parked outside. He'd noticed her lights were still on. Did she have a few minutes to talk to him?

Nervous butterflies filled Tansy's stomach as she waited for him to come up the stairs to her apartment. He'd sounded so serious on the phone that she couldn't help worrying. It had something to do with that woman. Who was she, and what impact did she have on Ian's life?

When she let him in, Ian's expression was so severe that she became even more nervous. What was wrong?

Everything had been so wonderful today. What could have happened?

He tore off his coat, and she steered him toward the couch, where he sank heavily. "The woman you saw at my house tonight is my mother," he said, his voice devoid of emotion.

"Oh," Tansy didn't know what else to say because Ian didn't seem happy about this situation. She sat down beside him. "You've never mentioned your mother. I didn't know she was still alive."

"I didn't, either," Ian said bitterly. "I haven't seen her in years."

"Oh." Tansy folded her hands in her lap to stop herself from hugging him. She knew she should leave him alone while he explained, but she longed to hold him and ease his pain. "Have Daniel or Mike spoken with her recently?"

Ian blew out a deep breath. "Tansy, I need to tell you something. A lot of things. I don't know what you'll think of me once I tell you, but I have to. It would be unfair not to."

A feeling of dread settled over Tansy. This didn't sound good at all. "I'm sure whatever it is, it's not as bad as you think."

His gaze met and held hers. She could see the pain in his eyes, could see how much he was suffering. "I hope so. Let me start by telling you something about Daniel and Mike. We aren't biological brothers."

Tansy tipped her head, trying to understand what he was saying. "So you were adopted?"

"We adopted each other. We met as teenagers. We'd all been arrested for various reasons, ended up briefly in juvenile detention, then in a series of foster homes, but we never lost touch. We were like brothers from the beginning, and when we got older, we decided to become brothers. We all changed our last name to Foster and decided to take care of each other like real brothers did. We eventually moved to the valley, and we've been here ever since."

Tansy had covered her shock well, she thought, but she couldn't hide her sadness for the young Ian. How terrible not to have family in your life. "I'm so glad you met Daniel and Mike," she said.

Ian looked disgusted with himself. "Didn't you hear the part about juvenile detention?"

She scooted closer to him and curled her hand around his wrist, unable to stop herself from touching him any longer. "I did. I also know you're a good person. Whatever you did, you had a reason for doing it. It also sounds like you paid for your mistakes."

He turned his head, and she could clearly see the years of anguish in his eyes. "It's okay, Ian. You were young. Tell me what happened."

He sighed. "My mother drank. A lot. And I never knew who my father was, much less where he was. She and I drifted from town to town. Sometimes she'd work, but most times, she was too drunk. When I got older, I took care of us. She'd often leave me alone for days. I had to take care of myself then. I'd do chores in whatever town we lived in. I'd walk to the nice neighborhoods and offer to rake leaves or mow lawns or shovel snow. As I got older, people started to be more afraid of me because my clothes were ratty and I couldn't afford haircuts. The jobs dried up. Then one day, my mother left and didn't come back. She was just gone. I tried to find a way to make a living, and I couldn't." He closed his eyes before continuing. "So I stole. I shoplifted food and clothes. I broke into houses looking for cash. Eventually I got caught."

Tansy couldn't keep the tears from running down her face. She held Ian close, trying to take away the pain. "I'm so sorry."

He hugged her back briefly, then moved away, standing and pacing her small living room. "So now my mother's back. Now, when I've worked so hard to build a new life for myself, she's come back. And I'm scared she's going to ruin everything."

Tansy could certainly understand why he would feel that way. The woman had been a terrible mother.

"You're strong now, Ian. You have people who love you. You're not a boy anymore," she said softly.

Ian nodded. "I know. That's what Daniel and Mike said. I spoke with them before I came over here. I wanted to let them know what might happen."

Tansy was trying to understand his concerns, but she wasn't quite following his point. "What do you think could happen?"

"For starters, my mother could tell everyone that she isn't Daniel's or Mike's mother, that we aren't really brothers."

Tansy shrugged. "No one will care. You're still brothers in every way that counts."

Ian's eyes told her he wanted to believe she was right. "I don't know," he said. "A lot of people may be angry at us for lying. And the problem is, I won't be the only one to suffer. Daniel and Mike will, too."

She wished she could convince him he was worrying about nothing. The valley might be small and gossipy, but its people were kind and tolerant—suspicious of strangers, yes, but they no longer considered the Foster brothers to be strangers.

"It won't matter to anyone, Ian," she argued. "They won't care how you came to be brothers. All they care about is that you're loved and respected here."

"It *will* matter that we met in juvenile detention," he said bleakly.

Tansy shook her head. "The good people will understand. You were a teenager, homeless, alone and starving. You did what you had to do to survive. You've paid for the past, and now you're a wonderful man. That's all that matters. You really are a wonderful man, Ian. Nothing your mother does can change that."

He pulled her up from the sofa and wrapped his arms around her. For a moment, they stood still, just holding each other. Then Ian said, "I hope you're right, because I told her she could stay for a few days. I don't want to regret that decision."

Tansy snuggled closer to him, wanting her love to heal his wounds. "You won't. I think it's great that you'll get to spend some time with her. Maybe she's changed. Maybe you and she can build some sort of relationship."

"I don't know. I have a bad feeling about it," Ian said, tucking her head under his chin. "But you could be right. I mean, a miracle has already happened tonight."

"What miracle?"

"I thought you'd reject me, send me packing—not

because of who I used to be, but because I've been living a lie."

"You should have trusted me all along," Tansy said, "but I'm so glad you decided to trust me now."

"IT'S BEAUTIFUL, TY," Tansy said to the young man who'd just set up a display of his hand-thrown pottery. It was museum-quality work. Ty was mentally challenged, but had found his calling when he took a pottery class at the special school he attended. Ty beamed, and so did his mother, who'd helped him cover his terraced display table with dark blue velveteen that emphasized the signature cobalt glaze of his bowls, pitchers and dinner plates.

The thought hummed through Tansy's mind that a little publicity for Ty might propel him to the top of his craft. She'd mention it to Martha.

"What's the likelihood of theft?" said the middle-aged designer of exquisite silver jewelry who'd scurried up to her, nervous and tight-lipped. "I have locked cases in the van if you think—"

"None whatever," Tansy said breezily. The woman had been a pain in the neck all morning, but her jewelry made up for it.

"Tansy, the place is gorgeous!" Allie said breathlessly. The reason for her breathlessness was easy enough to figure out. She'd blown through the door with an electric food warmer almost as big as she was, while Maury, Mike's sous-chef and soon-to-be-adopted son, carried two huge boxes as if they were butterflies.

"Thank the Decorations Committee."

Allie and Maury got right to work setting up the food

section, so Tansy had time to scan the main room of the Town Hall, bursting with pride at the setting the committee had accomplished. The tree, brilliantly lighted and dripping with tinsel and ornaments borrowed from the committee members, stood in a corner at the back. It had taken several strong men, a tall ladder and a bunch of risk-takers to set up that tree. She'd spent yesterday at the hall, enjoying the scene and simultaneously worrying about whether the town had some sort of insurance that would cover broken limbs and priceless antique ornaments, or if that sort of insurance even existed.

Wreaths hung high on the walls. Outside, lighted wreaths illuminated the front of the building, upstairs and downstairs. All that had required even taller ladders. More insurance worries.

A string of lights led to an even more brightly lighted doorway—no one could possibly miss the entrance, and an electric candle stood in each of Town Hall's many windows. "Our thanks to Lights Unlimited for providing..." was placed in a prominent position on the handout Myrtle Parsons would give to each attendee at the door, which also described each booth and its location in the hall.

Tansy sighed. The festival would be everything she'd dreamed it would be. And no one had suffered so much as a scratch. At least, not yet.

Her cell phone rang. It was Ian. She was glad to hear from him. He'd had a rough couple of days adjusting to his mother's presence in his house, so on Wednesday, she'd gone to dinner at his house and met his mother. The conversation had been somewhat stilted, but it was obvious the woman was trying.

Yesterday and this morning, she'd been busy setting up for the festival and hadn't seen Ian at all. She missed him and could hardly wait until he got to the hall.

"Hi, how are you?" she asked when she answered.

"Tansy," Ian said, "it's snowing like the dickens out here."

"Oh, no! The weather report said—"

"Forget the weather report. Look out the window."

Tansy was already on her way. What she saw outside was indeed snow, but fairly light. A quick sweep of the sidewalk and everything would be fine.

"No problem here," she said cheerfully.

"There will be in about a minute," Ian said. "It's coming in from the east."

He was right. In seconds, the snow got heavier. And heavier. "The town can't afford to plow until it stops," she said, as cold as if the snow were falling directly on her.

"I'm plowing my way into town right now to set up my booth—booths," he said, sounding determined.

"Is it going to turn into a disaster?" she wailed, but softly, just for Ian.

"Nope. I won't let it."

Just what she needed to hear.

"Tansy!" Martha was running across the hall, waving her cell. When she was close enough, she hissed, "Have you heard the news? The storm's right on top of us."

"It does look serious, doesn't it," Tansy said calmly. "Let me think. How should we attack the problem?"

"If we don't plow down from the point the state takes

care of," Martha said desperately, "nobody from out of town can get here. If we don't plow Holman and shovel the sidewalks, nobody from the valley can get up to the doors."

"Customarily," Tansy said, frowning, "we don't plow until the snow lets up, but we may have to make an exception. So let's see…" She drummed her fingers on the face of her own cell phone. "Here's how we'll start. I'll call the mayor of LaRocque and see if his road crew can plow down to our border."

"He'll do it," Martha said, looking a little less frantic, "because Ty and Ian's knitter are from LaRocque, and Ty's father's brother works on the—"

"Forget the family connections for now," Tansy said. "Our maintenance people can pick up from there and plow directly to Town Hall before they take care of the rest of the streets, because a lot of the townspeople can walk here. I'm sure Churchill is already working on the road across the bridge to LaRocque."

"You're on a roll," Martha said, then hesitated. "Your father," she added pointedly, "could get the road from the freeway to LaRocque's town line cleared with a single phone call."

"Oh, no," Tansy said. "I'm not going to pull political strings. It would bother my conscience *and* his. So I absolutely will not…excuse me," she said when her phone rang.

"Sweetheart," her father said when she answered, "you've got a problem here, so I called the—"

Tansy cringed, mumbled a few words of thanks, then ended the call. "I didn't have to ask. The state will clear for us immediately," she told Martha, feeling guilty as sin, "and the federal government is already working on I-91." At least that would also benefit the world outside Holman.

"Then," Martha said firmly—she was calm as a pond in summer now, "volunteers will clear the sidewalks and entrance to Town Hall."

"Which volunteers? They're all in here."

"Trust me," Martha said.

Within minutes, there were fewer people in the hall, and glancing out the window, Tansy saw the missing persons outside, shoveling vigorously.

Martha could be a pain in the neck, Tansy reflected, but she might make a darned good campaign manager.

Still looking out the window, she saw Ian arrive. He'd attached his plow to the front of his largest truck, and had protected his paintings with a fitted steel cover for the truck bed in back. She was at the front door to welcome him, and couldn't believe how many people spilled out of that truck.

Six people plus one ewe, who was the calmest of the lot. First Ian, who helped down a woman who looked as if she wished she were anywhere but here, then two of his farmhands, closely followed by Joe, who helped Edna out, and finally Tim.

Tansy couldn't take her eyes off the spectacle. Ian signed something to Tim which must have been to get Edna and Joe into the building, because that's what he did.

And after they were safely inside, being offered hot cider by a sympathetic Allie, Tim went back for the nervous woman, who stepped in saying, "I'm the spinner.

After my experience in a chauffeured snowplow, this had better be good."

While Tim was helping the woman—who turned out to be, in fact, a master-spinner who was donating her time—get cidered and settled, Ian and the farmhand began bringing in disaster-wrapped paintings. Tansy had just enough time to send Ian a look she hoped would convey her gratitude before a string of vans, trucks and cars crawled up to Town Hall in the wake of Ian's plowing. More craftspeople were arriving.

She glanced at the clock. The festival didn't open for three hours. With any luck, the roads would be cleared by then.

Feeling that the situation was temporarily under control, she sneaked over to Ian.

"How's it going with your mother," she asked.

"Okay." He gave her a small, reassuring smile. "No problems. We left her at home. She'll be fine there. And with the plow, I will get home, come hell or high water."

"With your spinner?" Tansy teased.

"What a pill," Ian groaned. "Yes, I invited her to come down yesterday and stay with us through the weekend."

"You're a saint."

"No," Ian said, "a pushover, which is all your doing."

"I'm still worried about the weather," Tansy admitted. "If it's even worse tomorrow— Oh, Ian, we've put so much effort into the festival."

"It'll work out," Ian told her. "Don't worry. Tomorrow is supposed to be a picture-postcard Vermont day, snow on the ground and sunshine. I'm off to set up," he said. "Think positive thoughts."

Yes, positive thoughts were definitely needed. And at six o'clock, they seemed to have worked, because people, familiar and unfamiliar, burst into the hall and the festival started with a bang.

Some went straight to Mike's cups of soup, breads and desserts, priced so low she knew Mike was taking a huge loss. But that was what the Foster brothers did, they gave and gave and gave, and now even Ian was offering not only money, but himself.

Others, predictably, headed for the booths of their relatives. Yes, family was important, but especially in Serenity Valley.

The visitors with children zeroed in on the "sheep to sweater" demonstration, moving wide-eyed from one wedge of the circular booth to the next. One of the farmhands was shearing the patient ewe, because Ian had his hands full. His art booth was mobbed. Valley residents she recognized as well as total strangers were lined up to get closer to the paintings. She was exulting in his success when a man blew through the front door. Irritably, he brushed snow off his otherwise impeccable dark suit and overcoat. Waving aside the festival guide, he approached Tansy. "Show me to Ian Foster's booth. Devon Townsend," he announced, as if he expected her to fall to her knees in adoration, "the Townsend Gallery in Boston."

"The line starts right there," she told him sweetly, pointing toward the queue, "and it will be worth the wait."

IAN WAS GLAD TO SEE THAT the weather on Saturday morning was clear. Frigid, but no new snow. Although the festival attendance last night had exceeded all expectations, considering the storm, today they anticipated record crowds. If this weather held, they should get their wish.

He hadn't had any time at all to talk to Tansy last night. He'd had customers and the simply curious to deal with. *And* the gallery owner from Boston. Forget how important he thought he was, how much he said he could do for Ian's career, he was about the most obnoxious person Ian had ever met and over his dead body would he turn over his paintings to the man.

Tansy had been busy running from booth to booth, checking for problems. Ian had wanted to stick around to help her close up last night, but he'd needed to get the spinner home, and settle down the disoriented ewe for the night.

He'd had to make do with a short phone conversation with her, not much, not enough, but just hearing her voice before he collapsed in bed was absolutely essential to his peace of mind.

"That…*vulture,*" he'd told her sleepily, "offered me twice the percentage of sales I'd get from any other gallery if I'd let him give me a show."

She sounded amused. "Well, Ian, that's not all bad."

"I'm not doing it. I was thinking…well, that Bunny person turned out to be pretty reasonable. I might consider…"

As he rolled out of bed this morning, he *was* considering a show in New York, and it suddenly seemed like something he could handle—as long as he didn't have to go there or meet anybody.

On his way to the kitchen, his cell rang. He glanced at the display, hoping it was Tansy, but it was Daniel. "Hey, Nick is feeling under the weather. Lilah and I want to take the rest of the kids and Jesse to the festival tomorrow. Think Edna would look after him for a couple of hours? We could drop him by your place."

Ian knew Edna adored Nick, but still he asked her before saying yes. As he'd known she would, Edna readily agreed, then started talking cocoa and chicken noodle soup.

That settled, Ian went to the guest room to check on his mother. So far, things had been going well, although he hadn't spent much time with her. Once the festival ended, he needed to rectify that.

He found her sitting on the neatly made bed, the guest room phone in her hand.

"Good morning," he said.

She glanced up at him. She looked sad. Really sad. Ian tensed. "Good morning," she said.

"Are you okay?"

She set the phone on the bedside table and stood up. She was wearing one of the outfits he'd had Edna buy for her the day after she'd arrived, casual trousers and a loose-fitting sweater. "Yes. I'm fine."

Ian knew something was wrong, and he braced himself. "What happened?"

His mother shook her head. "My friend, the one who drove me here, is sick. I'm a little worried about him." She smiled slightly, a smile that was obviously forced. "But I'm sure he'll be all right."

Ian didn't know what to say, and he also had to get going. People were counting on him.

"We can talk tonight," he told his mother. "I hope your friend recovers."

His mother nodded. "Yes. I hope so, too. And don't worry about me."

But as Ian walked away he realized he *was* worried about her, and he had been since she'd reappeared in his life. And worse, he still didn't trust her.

Chapter Twelve

On Saturday, Town Hall was so jammed that Ian saw Tansy and the selectpersons in a head-shaking huddle, probably worried about fire codes. The scents of coffee and hot spiced cider, Mike's special cinnamon rolls and Vermont-style cake doughnuts permeated the room. Visitors strolled from booth to booth, eating, drinking—and buying.

With one ear, Ian caught bits of gossip. The three valley bed-and-breakfasts were sporting big no-vacancy signs. In response to pleas from the Chamber of Commerce, numerous private homes had become impromptu bed-and-breakfasts for the weekend. Ty's pottery had been "discovered."

And Ian had also been discovered.

When he'd had it with compliments and art dealers fawning over him, Tansy rescued him and took over his art display. With great relief, he retreated to the "sheep to sweater" demonstration, doing the shearing himself. At last, it was closing time.

"You look like a patchwork quilt," he told the ewe, stroking her. "Just one more day, and it will be over.

You've been a really good sport. When we get home, I'm going to give you a special treat."

"Ian."

He looked up to see Tansy's father looking at him, and at the sheep, and at him talking to the sheep.

"Senator," he said, shaking the man's hand.

"Roger, please. Very interesting demonstration you have here," Roger said, still examining the sheep. "Lot of interest in your paintings, too." He glanced around the crowded Town Hall. Most booths still had healthy lines in front of them. By now, visitors were spooning soup out of cups, or eating small overstuffed sandwiches, or forking up wedges of pie—even though the festival was closing in a few minutes. "Looks like you had an excellent turnout."

"Yep. It's been good. I think Tansy is happy, and we still have tomorrow to go." Ian nodded toward the back of the hall where she was speaking to a group of people at his booth. "She's great at this."

Roger turned to face him. "Yes, she is. And it would be a terrible thing to keep her from reaching her potential, or do anything that could harm her career."

Ian stiffened, not liking where this conversation was going. "I'd never stand in Tansy's way," he said.

The older man seemed unconvinced. "Maybe not intentionally, but politics is a funny line of work. You can get into a real mess if you associate with the wrong sort of people."

Ian gritted his teeth. "Meaning?"

"Meaning I stopped by your house the other day to see if Tansy was there. Instead, I had the chance to meet your lovely mother. We had a nice little chat.

She explained that both she—and you—have had some trouble in the past."

Ian struggled through a wave of anger and anxiety. This was exactly what he'd feared. His mother had begun talking at her first opportunity. Now the valley would find out about him—and his brothers.

"That was a long time ago. I was a kid," Ian said.

Roger shrugged. "I'm not judging you. These things happen. Don't worry," he added. "I won't tell anybody. I hope you've told Tansy."

Ian could only nod.

"I'm sure she was very sympathetic, because she's a sensitive person, but, Ian, you have to understand what your history could do to her dreams. Despite what she said at lunch the other day, she's always wanted to run for state office. She's talked about it for years, and your background could really cost her."

Ian started to speak, but what could he say? Roger was right. He'd be kidding himself if he didn't acknowledge that his past could haunt Tansy.

"Something to think about," Roger said. He walked away without a backward glance.

Ian looked across the room at Tansy, who was smiling and chatting with the crowd. He felt empty inside. Cold. Her father was right. She deserved a better man than him. She deserved a chance to fulfill her dreams.

She was the last person in the world he wanted to hurt.

"You need to do everything you can to ensure that whoever paints the Town Hall understands restoration. Check references and ask around," Martha said, her arms crossed over her ample bosom. "This is important, Tansy."

Exhausted, more than ready to go home and fall into bed, Tansy kept her smile firmly tacked in place and nodded. Did the woman honestly think she was going to hire an unknown off the street?

"Yes, I know it's important, Martha," she said. "The town will take bids and check references before deciding."

"Good, because with all the crafts, not to mention Ian's wonderful paintings raising so much money, we'll be able to do the job right." Martha's expression turned smug. "I knew all along that his paintings would bring in a lot of visitors. Didn't I tell you?"

Um, no she hadn't. In fact, Martha had been rather negative about Ian's paintings, at least until the reporter arrived and pointed out how good they were. But Tansy wasn't petty enough to call the older woman on her faulty memory.

"You're right. Ian's paintings are wonderful," Tansy said, looking at the display. With Sunday still ahead of them, two-thirds of his paintings already had Sold tags.

"I've always felt Ian was a special man," Martha said. "A real asset to the town."

Okay, that was too much. Tansy barely managed to contain her laughter at Martha's last statement. The older woman had never liked Ian and had been quite vocal about it over the years. Now, because he could paint and was making a lot of money for the town, he was Martha's best friend.

While Tansy struggled to come up with a response,

she noticed her father making his way toward her. After he'd greeted Martha, he smiled broadly at Tansy.

"Great work on this project," he said, giving her a bear hug.

Tansy hugged him back. "Thanks, Dad. But I only did a small part. The town really pulled this together. Everyone has worked so hard."

"Well, that's what a leader does," Roger said. He waited until a volunteer drew Martha away, then said, "A great leader sets the stage for success but always gets others involved, as well. This is just one more example of why you'll make a great senator one day."

Tansy took a step away from him. "Dad, I don't know if I want to do that. I'm happy where I am at the moment, and you need to stop pushing me."

Her father frowned. Then, as though someone had flicked a light switch, he smiled. "Of course. No pressure. I just want you to keep an open mind. I'm a proud father who wants to see his daughter succeed. You've spent many years talking about running for higher office. I want to see it happen."

The crowded Town Hall wasn't the place for this discussion, but Tansy realized she'd have to address it at some point. Her father couldn't go around making plans for her future. What she did—or didn't do—with her future was her choice.

Trying to lighten the mood, she asked, "Where's Mom?"

"Home with a cold, I'm afraid. I should be getting back to her. But I wanted to wish you well," he said, still smiling. "Oh, and I also said hello to Ian. I got to meet his mother this week. Have you met her yet?"

Tansy froze. "You met Ian's mother? When?"

Roger glanced around the room, obviously nonchalant. It was clear to Tansy that he had an agenda. "Hmm? Oh, I stopped by the other day looking for you and ran into Cheryl." He paused, then added, "Interesting woman. Sad past."

Anger raced through Tansy, but because they were in a public place, she tapped it down. "But it is her *past,* Dad." She tried to catch her father's eye, knowing the real meaning of his words. "And his years with his mother are part of Ian's past."

He shrugged, still scanning the room and avoiding looking directly at Tansy. "True. But she told me a few things that concerned me since my daughter is dating her son. When I checked—"

Tansy's fury broke free. "You ran a background check on Ian's mother?"

Her father looked at her now, his expression stern. "Keep your voice down, Tansy."

Even though they were by themselves in a small alcove, people might stroll by and hear. Tansy didn't want that happening any more than her father did.

"You had no right to do that," she said.

"I didn't do a formal check, just a little research. His mother has been in and out of jail a few times, mostly for alcohol-related charges. I also found some very disturbing information about Ian's teenage years, trouble with the law, that sort of thing."

"As I said, that was in the past," she snapped. She wasn't a child. She was capable of making her own decision about the man.

Her father must have noticed her reaction, but his

calm, matter-of-fact voice rolled on as if he hadn't. "His last name used to be O'Donnell. Not really sure what happened there, but I guess his mother married at some point, and Ian was adopted by his stepfather. It's odd that I didn't find any information about his brothers. I thought you should know. Tread carefully, Tansy. Whether you plan to run for higher office or not, you need to be sure about whomever you associate with. Even as mayor, you can't afford to be linked with—"

Finally, Tansy interrupted. "With what, Dad? A wonderful man? The first man I've ever dated who loves me for me and not for what he thinks I can get you to do for him?"

Her father sighed and rubbed one hand across his forehead. "Tansy, I just want you to be happy. I'm like any other dad. I worry about my children. I don't mean to upset you, and I didn't mean to upset Ian earlier when I—"

Tansy held up a hand. "Wait. You spoke to Ian about this?"

Before her father could answer, Tansy scanned the room. She spotted Ian packing up his things.

"We'll talk later, Dad," she said, moving rapidly toward Ian.

She needed to make certain he didn't pay any attention to her father. Roger Appletree might be a smart man, but he was all wrong about Ian.

When she was partway across the hall, Ian answered his cell phone. After a moment, he spun around and headed toward the door. He stopped for only a second to talk to Daniel on his way out, then both men rushed away.

Tansy's anger at her father disappeared to be replaced

by fear. She searched the crowd. Lilah was talking on her cell, too, and obviously upset.

A sickening feeling settled in Tansy's stomach. Something really bad had happened. She dashed out the door to catch up with Ian.

NICK WAS MISSING. IAN couldn't believe it. Edna had been so happy to be taking care of him. Nick had seemed delighted to spend a sick day with her. But Edna had just called to tell him she'd looked everywhere for him. He'd gone down the hall to see Cheryl, and suddenly he raced past Edna and out the front door.

There was more bad news. When she went to Cheryl's room to see what might have happened, she found Ian's mother drunk.

Now Ian and Tansy were on their way to the farm, while Daniel traced the path from his house to Ian's in case Nick had decided to run home to safety.

His mother had struck again. Ian should have known better than to think she'd changed. She'd been at his house for only four days and already she'd blabbed to Tansy's father and had caused Nick to run away.

Nick was out there alone in the dark and the cold. If anything happened to that boy, Ian would never forgive himself. Even though Edna was watching Nick, his mother was in the same house. Hadn't he learned anything as a kid? Cheryl O'Donnell was not to be trusted.

"Ian, I'm so sorry," Tansy said, putting her hand on his arm. "But I'm sure we'll find him."

Having Tansy with him helped him calm down. She'd caught up with him in the parking lot and insisted on coming along. "Should I get the police involved?" She sounded as anxious as he felt. "I could make a call."

"Not yet. Getting picked up by the police would scare him to death. Let me try to find him first. If I can't within the next half hour, we'll call the sheriff."

"I hope it doesn't come to that." She paused for a second, both of them lost in their thoughts. When he turned up the small road that led to his farm, she said softly, "I love you, Ian."

His heart constricted at her words. He loved her, too, but sometimes loving someone wasn't enough. He'd loved his mother as a child, but he hadn't been able to save her. He loved Nick, but now he'd failed to protect the already fragile boy.

And he loved Tansy, but he realized that he could ruin her life.

So rather than say the words he knew she wanted to hear, he said, "I know. It helps." It was all he could manage at the moment. He needed to focus on Nick. He had to find the boy.

He called Joe and asked him to summon the hands that weren't at the festival and tell them to start looking. When they reached the house, he and Tansy ran inside. Edna met them in the hallway, crying.

"I don't know what happened. I was making biscuits for him because you know how he loves my biscuits. He was talking about your paintings and how he wants to be like you when he grows up. Then he went to get your mother so she could have dinner with us and see how good my biscuits are, and..." She wiped her eyes. "I came out of the kitchen after a couple of minutes to look for him and found the front door open and your mother—" She frowned and pointed toward Ian's office. "She's in there."

Ian hugged her quickly. "We'll find him. Don't worry."

He glanced at Tansy, who stayed with Edna, then stalked toward his office. He braced himself as he opened the door. He found his mother, obviously drunk, thumbing through the envelope of cash he kept in his desk. She was stuffing the bills into her pocket when she noticed him and quickly shoved the envelope back into the drawer.

"Oh, hi, Ian." She smoothed her hair. "How was your carnival thing?"

All of the pain Ian had felt growing up returned full force. He wanted to yell at her, wanted to tell her how much he hated her for everything she'd done to him. But instead he simply asked, "What did you say to Nick?"

His mother shook her head. "Nothing. I was upset because my friend is very sick. So I had a small drink. Nothing much. Just one…and then I was still upset, so I was having another small drink when that boy came in. He looked at me and ran away. I don't know why. I didn't say a word to him. I was very nice. I smiled at him."

Sure, and that made Nick feel a lot better—so much better that he ran away. "I'll talk to you later about the money you just stole. Go pack. You'll be leaving as soon as I find Nick."

He stormed out of the office and ran into Tansy. "Can you and Edna check the whole house, the closets, the attic, in case Nick changed his mind and came back? He might be hiding in here."

The women set off, Tansy to the upstairs, Edna to the downstairs bedrooms, as Ian went outside.

"We've scoured the barns and the bunkhouse," Joe told him, sounding panicked, "and the boys are going over it again. But we can't find any footprints leading away from the house." Joe pointed at the fresh-fallen snow. "So either he's somewhere near here, or he walked down the road to get back to Daniel's."

Ian nodded. "Daniel's tracing the road from town. You guys just keep looking."

Where would Nick go? He yelled his name a couple of times, but there was no answer.

"Did you try my studio?" he asked.

Joe nodded. "First thing." Other than the barn and the house, the only other place Nick had been on the farm was the pond. He started to head that way but stopped. He stared at the barn for a long moment, unable to shake a feeling.

"Check the pond," he told Joe. "He went skating there last week. I'm going to take another look in the studio."

THE BIG ROOM WAS QUIET when Ian walked inside and flipped on the overhead light. A quick glance around proved Nick was nowhere to be seen.

But Ian hadn't expected to see him. Instead, he walked over to the small closet tucked in the far corner where he kept canvases and supplies. Most people would never notice it, but Nick knew it was there.

Holding his breath, Ian opened the door, relief flooding through him when he found Nick scrunched up inside. He wanted to gather the little boy into his arms, but he also didn't want to distress him any more than his mother already had, so he said, "Hi, Nick. You've had us all worried."

Nick sniffed, making it clear he'd been crying. "Sorry. I just got…scared."

Ian walked quickly over to the studio door and hollered out to Tim and the hands that he'd found Nick. Then he came back over and sat on the floor near the boy.

"What happened, buddy? Can you tell me about it?"

"That lady, your mother, was crying and stuff. When I went to ask if she was okay, she looked at me. Her eyes were all red, and she smelled bad. She smelled like…" He sat for a moment, then said in a voice so faint Ian could hardly hear him. "Like some other people I used to know."

Ian froze. Nick had never told anyone what had happened to him. Despite the therapy Daniel had gotten for him, the little boy had insisted he didn't remember. He'd been found on the back stoop of a woman's house disoriented and confused, and he'd never volunteered a word about how he ended up there.

"I'm sorry she frightened you, Nick. My mother… has problems," Ian said. "I thought she was better when I asked her to stay for a few days, but now I see she's not. I'm going to get her the help she needs."

Nick nodded, then wrapped his arms around his bony knees. "She's a nice lady. She didn't yell at me or anything. She isn't mean like my mother was."

"You remember your mother?" Ian asked. His heart was thudding. This was a breakthrough. It was the most important moment of the boy's life, and Ian had to choose his own words carefully to keep him talking.

Nick nodded. "And my dad. I just didn't want to talk about them." His eyes shone with tears. "I was afraid somebody would find them and make me go back."

Ian put his arm around the boy's shoulder. "I promised you I'd never let you go away with anyone unless you wanted to. Remember?"

Nick nodded.

"Would you like to tell me about your parents?" Ian asked quietly, "since you know I'd never try to find them?"

"She used to be like your mother." Nick burst into sobs. "She'd have that smell on her breath, and she'd get real mad at me and hit me sometimes. So would my dad."

Ian gathered him closer. "It's okay, buddy. I'm so sorry."

"They would leave me alone and go away. I was scared, but they'd get mad when they got home and saw me crying." After such a long silence, the story was spilling out of the boy. He rubbed his hands over his eyes and went on. "They were really mad one day, so they took me to a park and gave me lots of medicine. I fell asleep. When I woke up, it was dark and I was scared."

Ian realized tears had welled up in his own eyes. He wanted to find these people and make certain they were punished but, more important, he wanted to help Nick.

"I'm sorry, Nick. I'm so sorry," he said.

"I walked around for a long time until I ended up

outside some lady's house. She called the police and gave me some real good food while I waited for them, and then they took me to Daniel's house." He turned his tear-streaked face toward Ian. "What if they come back? What if they kidnap me?"

Ian's heart was breaking for the little guy. Although his mother had never hit him, she'd left him lots of times and finally, forever. He knew the terror Nick had felt, and at that very moment, decided he'd make sure Nick never returned to that life.

"You won't ever have to live with them again," he told Nick. "In fact, what would you think about living here with me?"

Nick's sobs faded away. He looked at Ian, but without much hope. "You mean it?"

Yes, he meant it. It was what he wanted to do. What he *would* do. "I'd like to adopt you if you'd be willing to adopt me."

Nick's miserable face lit up. "You'd really do that?"

"I sure would, no matter how much stuff we'll have to do to make it happen." And he wanted Tansy to be Nick's mother, but he realized now it was something he couldn't have.

"There are just two things." He gazed at the boy. "You have to accept that I'll always be here for you. I'll make sure you're safe, so you have to promise me you'll never, ever run away again. If you feel bad about anything, talk to me about it."

Nick said solemnly, "I promise. What's the other thing?"

"I'd like you to call me Dad instead of Uncle Ian."

Nick gave him a brilliant smile and breathed, "I've got a dad!"

He flung his arms around Ian. Ian carried him out of the closet, and in the big studio, whirled him around and around until the room rang with Nick's laughter.

He was so full of love he'd had to do something. Nick had a dad, and he had a son.

TANSY STOOD OUTSIDE THE DOOR to the studio, anxiously waiting until she could go inside. She wanted to give Ian time to talk with Nick, but she was worried about the little boy. He'd been through so much.

When the silence turned into boisterous sound, she couldn't resist anymore. She slowly opened the door and peered down to see Ian spinning Nick through the air.

"Hi, guys," she said.

Ian came to a stop, then grinned. "Nick's okay now."

Tansy nodded and smiled. "So I see."

Nick ran up the stairs and grabbed her hand, tugging her down to where Ian stood. "Uncle Ian's going to adopt me! I'm going to have a dad of my own!"

Tears formed in Tansy's eyes as she looked at Ian. "That's wonderful."

Ian shrugged. "He's a great kid. I'm pretty lucky."

They were both great guys, and Tansy was very glad they had each other.

The three of them returned to the house. When Edna had hugged Nick all he'd let her, Ian gave the boy a serious look. "I have to talk to my mother about how she scared you. Stay here with Tansy and Edna for a while."

"The cocoa's hot." Edna enticed Nick when he seemed unwilling to let go of Ian's hand.

Tansy eyed the two of them wistfully. She was so grateful that Ian had found Nick safe, and thrilled that they were forming a family. She wanted to be part of that family, but she knew that for now, Ian would need to concentrate on building a life with his new son. Maybe once things settled down, they could see where their own relationship was going.

She hoped so.

IAN FOUND HIS MOTHER sitting in his office where he'd left her. She looked better, but he knew she was still drunk.

"You have to leave tonight. You can go to a clinic and get help, or you can go back where you came from. But you can't stay here," he said flatly.

Cheryl's eyes filled with tears. "I didn't mean to do it, Ian. I've been sober for months. But today I found out my friend Burt is dying. It made me very sad, and so I had a little something to ease the pain, you know?"

Ian shook his head. "No, I don't know. I don't have any liquor in the house. That means you brought it here. I can't have you in my life if you don't get treatment. Too much is at stake. You talked to Tansy's father when I asked you not to talk to anyone. You frightened Nick. I can't have you around him."

He braced himself for the stream of excuses he knew would come. Nothing was ever her fault. But this time, all she said was, "I'd get help if I could, but those rehab places cost a lot."

"I'll pay for it," Ian told her. "But you have to do your

part, too. If you can't be rehabilitated, then you have to get out of my life and never see me again."

As much as Ian wanted to believe that she'd change, he wasn't sure. Only time would tell. He'd get her all the help he could, but the rest would be up to her.

"Then I'd like to try. I want to get better, Ian. I really do. I'm sorry I took your money," she said, timidly handing it back. "I guess I thought I could take a bus back to Burlington, see what I could do for Burt."

Ian took the cash, knowing that even if she'd bought a bus ticket, some of it would have been spent on alcohol. "I'm going to talk to Tansy now," he said gruffly. "She might be able to suggest a place for you."

His mother gave him a sad smile. "Thank you, Ian. You won't regret it. I promise. And Tansy won't, either. Her father tells me she's quite something. Going to go far, right? She sounds like a great person. I liked her."

"She's very special," Ian agreed. He left his mother in his office and went back to the kitchen to talk to Tansy. He realized there was one more conversation he had to have after he took care of his mother, a conversation that would end his hopes and dreams, and he was dreading it.

The time had come to face reality. Having him in her life could destroy Tansy's career. He loved her too much to let that happen, so even though it killed him, he would have to break things off.

It was the best—the only—thing to do.

Chapter Thirteen

Tansy glanced out her apartment window for what had to be the twentieth time in the past ten minutes. Ian should be here soon.

On Sunday, she'd manned Ian's booth for him, and one of the hands had returned to shear the sheep. She'd stayed late, her mind not on what she was doing, to accept—and give—compliments on the festival's success. Today, she'd helped Ian make arrangements for his mother to enter a treatment facility. She'd stayed with Nick while he'd taken Cheryl there and gotten her settled. Then he'd driven Tansy back to the Town Hall so she could pick up her car while he dropped Nick at Daniel's house and broke the happy news about his adoption plans to his family. Through it all he'd been quiet, not touching her, but he'd said he'd stop by later so they could talk.

So now she was waiting for him to arrive. She had many things to be happy about—the huge success of the festival, Ian and Nick—but she didn't have a good feeling about this conversation. Even though he'd let her help him through the crisis with his mother, she hadn't forgotten what her father had done. She'd bet anything that Ian hadn't, either, and this talk was probably about that very subject.

When she heard him climbing the stairs to her apartment, she didn't feel the usual excitement. At the moment, all she felt was dread.

The serious expression on his face when she opened the door did nothing to relieve that dread.

"How did it go at Daniel's?" she asked, after he'd taken off his coat and joined her on the couch.

"Great. He's going to put me in touch with the right people to steer me through the adoption process. It will take some time, but Nick and I don't care. We know it'll all work out eventually." His mouth twisted in a wry smile. "I offered him a chance to take back his real first name. He told me he never wants to be Billy Siebold again. He wants to be Nick Foster."

Tansy was touched, and was about to say so, but Ian shifted on the couch so he was facing her and said, "We need to talk, Tansy."

Hoping to avert disaster, Tansy jumped in. "Ian, if this is about my father, you have to ignore him. I know what I want, and I want to be with you. You made a mistake when you were a child. It's not going to hurt my political chances any more than it will stop you from being able to adopt Nick."

Ian sighed, and she saw the sadness in his eyes. "Don't you see, that's part of the problem. Even if my background doesn't hurt your political future, what about Nick? He and I need time to adjust to being a family. He's been through a lot. I can't let him be dragged into a media circus, which you know will happen if you run for senate. The opposition will grab on to anything to damage your credibility. I could take it if they dug into my background. You could probably take it, as well. But, Tansy, what if they dig up Nick's story? What if they find his parents?"

"Oh, no." Tears pooled in Tansy's eyes. She hadn't expected this. She'd been prepared to argue that Ian's past wouldn't matter, regardless of what her future held. Even though Nick's background was even more irrelevant and any reputable opponent wouldn't mention it, the chance still existed that Nick could be hurt.

"Nick needs time now and help to realize his bad times are over, Tansy. He also needs me. Daniel has so many boys already that he doesn't have enough time for one-on-ones with Nick. I do. I have both time and the resources to get him the help he needs, and I can give him the calm, structured, loving home he deserves. I can't turn my back on him. He needs me."

But I need both of you! Her silent, anguished wail came from deep inside her. Her voice trembling, she said, "What if I stop right here at being mayor, or drop out of politics entirely?"

Ian slowly shook his head. "You love it, and if you gave up what you love, you'd come to resent me. We need to be realistic here. I need to focus on Nick at the moment. You need to focus on your future and deciding what you want. Being together just doesn't make sense for either of us at the moment."

Tansy tried to fight down her tears. "But I love you, Ian."

Ian gathered her close and kissed her softly. It was a kiss filled with affection, but also regret. "I know. I love you, too. But sometimes love just isn't enough, Tansy. This is one of those times."

He kissed her forehead then stood. Tansy stayed where she was on the couch. She couldn't watch him leave, so she closed her eyes, holding the tears back. She heard him put on his coat, then for a long moment, she heard nothing until, finally, she heard the door to her apartment open.

And close.

IAN STOOD IN HIS STUDIO staring out the window. The weather outside was sunny, although cold, but he sure didn't feel sunny. He was miserable. In fact, he was pretty sure he could be the poster boy for Miserable, Inc. The past week without Tansy had nearly killed him. He missed her so much.

"Dad?"

Ian turned and managed a smile for Nick. That part of his life did make him happy, very happy. He'd started the paperwork for the adoption and could hardly wait until he was Nick's legal father.

"Yeah, buddy."

Nick pointed to his painting. "What do you think?"

Ian studied the work. The child psychologist who was working with Nick encouraged him to express his emotions through his art, and the little boy was doing just that. The picture made Ian smile. It was so much more upbeat than anything he'd done before.

The painting was of a snowperson—a snowchild— who wore a bright red knit hat exactly like the one Nick wore all the time. It was standing on the pond at

Ian's farm, and you could tell by looking at it that it felt loved.

It made Ian want to cry.

"Great work, Nick," he said. "It's terrific."

Nick studied his painting. "I like it, too. Can I give it to Tansy? When is she going to come see us?"

Ian hadn't known exactly what to say to Nick about Tansy, so he'd explained that both he and Tansy were very busy at the moment. He'd hoped Nick hadn't noticed her absence.

Which was dumb. Of course Nick had noticed. He missed Tansy.

So did Ian.

Knowing he should be honest with Nick, Ian explained, "Tansy and I aren't dating anymore."

Nick frowned. "But she was in love with you. Her eyes got all sparkly when she looked at you. She let you kiss her."

"I know. And I loved her, too. But we want different things out of life. She has plans and maybe will become a state senator one day." Ian tried to sound matter-of-fact so Nick would see it as a good thing, but the boy kept frowning.

"Is it because of me?" Nick finally asked.

Ian hadn't expected that, and immediately reassured him. "Absolutely not, Nick. Tansy loves you very much. But she understands that right now, you and I need to spend time together."

Nick shrugged. "So let's spend time together with her, too. You're so sad when she's not here, Unc—Dad. I'm sad, too. Let's ask her to come back."

Ian shook his head. "It's not that easy. Remember I

said that she might want to become a senator someday? Well, people who do jobs like that are in the papers a lot. Reporters like to write about them and their families. I don't want anyone writing about me. I don't like being in the paper."

Nick touched his arm. "Are you afraid they'll say bad things about you?"

Although Ian knew he was handling this badly, Nick had managed to figure out the problem. "A little. But mostly, I just like living my life here on the farm without a lot of people around."

Nick didn't say anything for a moment. Instead, he looked at his snowperson painting. When he finally turned back to Ian he said, "Dr. Phelps says you can't let people push you around. If someone hurts your feelings, you have to get over it. And if they do something mean, it's not your fault. She says you can't be afraid all the time. I think she's right. I think you should be brave, Dad. I'm brave. If those reporters write about me, I won't pay any attention to what they say. What matters is that people love you and that you love them back. I love you, Dad. I love Tansy, too."

Dr. Phelps was the child psychologist Nick saw twice a week. Apparently she was a very smart woman.

"Nick, I just don't know." But Ian felt a glimmer of hope. Could they really make this work if they tried? Had he given up too easily? Both Daniel and Mike had come close to losing the women they loved through a lack of confidence in themselves. Was he doing the same thing?

"Don't let people push you around," Nick repeated, patting Ian's arm. "You should marry Tansy."

Ian gazed thoughtfully at Nick. "I should, should I?"

Nick nodded. "She makes you happy, and you make her happy. When we were at Daniel's house last night I heard Lilah telling Daniel that Tansy was very sad. I told them you were sad, too. You should make her happy."

Tansy was sad? That broke Ian's heart.

Nick was right. He'd spent too much of his life hiding. He'd hidden from his past, and the last thing he wanted Nick to do was the same thing. It was about time to move forward.

"I blew it, didn't I?"

"Big-time," Nick agreed, then sighed.

"I found the treasure I was looking for and wasn't man enough to hang on to it. I'm not sure Tansy will come back even if I ask her," Ian admitted.

"You could at least try," Nick said. "You could talk to her."

True. Talking was good, but it wasn't Ian's strongest skill. "What would I say?"

"What about, 'I really acted dumb and I'm sorry.'"

"I'd have to be a little more eloquent than that," Ian said.

Nick crinkled his nose. "What's *eloquent?*"

"It means you can say a lot of big words fast and with a lot of feeling."

"Oh." Nick thought about it. "You paint eloquent."

Ian was too stunned to inform Nick that he should have said *eloquently.* He felt a buzzing in his ears, remembering something Daniel had said: *You paint the feelings you can't let out any other way.*

"Thanks, buddy," he said. "Why don't we go in for a snack..."

"I will," Nick said, "but you need to stay here in your studio." He gave Ian a pointed look. "You have stuff to do, and I don't want to bother you."

Wonderingly, Ian gazed at him. "How old are you, anyway? Seven going on forty?"

Nick shot him an appreciative smile as he stood up. "I know a few things. I'm a smart kid."

"Yes," Ian said, "you are smart. Smarter than your dad."

"See you later," Nick said, "and, Dad, the smartest thing you could do is paint fast."

FOR A FEW MINUTES AFTER Nick left, Ian just stood still, thinking. He glanced at Nick's painting, then an image formed in his mind. His body moved like molasses as he took down the canvas resting on his easel and replaced it with a new one. He stared at it, thinking first about color. A little softer for this one, not quite as bold as the shades in his other paintings. The brush strokes a little gentler. The image more realistic.

He gazed at himself in the antique mirror he'd hung at the bottom of the stairwell so he could see who might be coming down to interrupt him. No, that would be the hardest part of the picture. He'd start with the easiest. Picking up his brush with hands that were none too steady, he got to work.

HOW HAD SOMETHING SO RIGHT gone so wrong? Tansy had made her decision, that she and Ian had to be together even if it meant giving up her career in politics immediately. And that she couldn't miss raising Nick.

At the same time, Ian had made his decision, that

he didn't want to be involved with a politician, that the publicity wouldn't be good for Nick.

She'd had a chance at love—real, honest, all-consuming love—and she'd lost it. She should have tried harder to change Ian's mind, to find another solution. Tears streamed down her face. That had been happening a lot in the past week.

Tansy was working at home, soliciting bids from painters for the Town Hall job they'd do in the spring. As she put down the phone, it rang.

"You need to have a cheery lunch with Lilah and me," Allie said. "No arguments. Meet us at Mike's in thirty minutes."

Tansy blinked. Not many options in that kind of invitation. She exchanged her ratty old bathrobe for leggings and a long beige sweater—that's how she felt today, beige—threw on the first coat she came across, and left for her "cheery" lunch.

"How've you been?" Allie asked while Tansy was still struggling out of her coat.

She paused in her struggle with one arm free and the other sticking straight out into the space between their table and the next.

"I've been okay. Well, maybe not exactly okay." At their doubting looks, she said, "I've been miserable."

"What happened?" Lilah said. "You and Ian were so happy, then suddenly…"

It was absolutely none of their business, so naturally she began to tell them everything. "Then suddenly we began to wonder if our lifestyles were compatible. I decided they were, but he decided they weren't. Thank you," she said when Lilah handed her a tissue. "He's worried about Nick and the media attention politicians get and all that, which makes him a great guy, so how can I argue with him?"

"I'm sorry," Allie said, patting her arm. "He's unhappy, too."

Lilah nodded. "I've never seen him so sad. He's too sad to be grumpy, even."

Tansy didn't like hearing that Ian was suffering. It made her even sadder. "Would you switch places with me, Lilah, so my back's to the room?"

"Of course."

"I mean," Tansy went on after they'd resettled, "Ian's right. Nick has to come first. But I just wish…" She looked blurrily at Lilah. "Do you have another tissue?"

Lilah handed her the pack. "So if he admitted he'd been wrong, you'd forgive him?"

"Did he say that? Did he tell you what he's feeling?" A little flutter of hope formed inside Tansy.

Lilah quirked up an eyebrow. "Has Ian ever told anyone what he was feeling?"

"All he told Mike and Daniel was that he'd realized he could be a serious drawback to your career and that Nick could get hurt," Allie said.

"He made that ridiculous decision because he was thinking it was the best thing for you, Tansy, and for Nick," Lilah said.

"Nick," Tansy said, and buried her head in her hands. "I miss Nick almost as much as I miss Ian. I wanted to be his mother. I wanted to be the best mother any little boy ever had."

"But you're saying you would take Ian back," Lilah said, "if he asked."

Tansy noticed that Lilah seemed to be speaking very carefully. It was, after all, a touchy point. "Yes," she said through her tears.

"You realize," Allie said just as carefully as Lilah, "that for Ian nothing will do but marriage, a lifetime commitment, a—"

"That's what I want, too," Tansy confessed. A moment passed, then she raised her head and said with a massive sniff. "Have you noticed nobody has waited on us? That's unusual."

"Colleen was waiting for the right moment," Allie said, "and I think this is it. You need the blue plate special, chicken and dumplings, and a great big piece of banana cream pie. That will stop you from crying."

"WHATCHA THINK?" IAN ASKED.

Nick tilted his head to one side. "It's great. But it needs a baby."

Ian whirled toward the boy. "A baby?"

"Yeah," Nick said. "Daniel and Lilah are having a baby, and it's all right with everybody."

"You're saying it would be all right with you?"

"Yep," Nick said, "so call me when you've fixed it."

Ian's eyes followed Nick up the steps. Right now, he didn't know how he'd survived all these years without him.

"SO HOW AM I GOING TO do this?" Ian said, worried. "I know she won't come here. I thought of the restaurant, but she sure isn't going to go to dinner with me."

He was in the studio with his whole family surrounding him, the very image of a group with their thinking caps on. "We could kidnap her," Allie said.

Ian gave her a look.

"Or tell her she should at least make an appearance at your deathbed," Mike offered.

"It's not funny," Ian said. "This is the most serious moment of my life."

"Of course it is," Daniel said soothingly. "Lilah, got any ideas?"

"Well, just one."

"Spill it," Ian said.

"Martha can help us," Lilah said. "She'll call Tansy, and—"

"Martha Latham?" Ian sputtered. "She'll bring the press with her."

"No, she won't," Lilah said. "I'm thinking Martha, because she has such a, well, a commanding voice. You might even call her bossy."

Ian snorted.

"Hush and listen to my plan."

TANSY WAS SO DEPRESSED she was ironing and watching sitcoms. Four cotton shirts were crisply rustling at her from the various doorknobs on which she'd hung them to dry completely, and Sitcom Dad had just informed Sitcom Daughter that she couldn't go to the prom in a silver lamé micro-miniskirt. When the phone rang, her heart, as always, surged with hope, then sank when Martha Latham's voice came across loud and clear.

"Tansy, could you get over to Town Hall? The janitor called me, and there's a leak upstairs. I'd go, but my family's here for dinner."

"There's no plumbing upstairs yet," Tansy said dully. "It has to be snow coming through the roof. I can't climb up there with a roll of duct tape and fix it. It will have to wait."

"You should at least check on it," Martha huffed. "You *are* the mayor."

Tansy silently groaned. "Okay, I'll go right now, see what's going on and call somebody."

At least that would be slightly more exciting than finding out what Sitcom Daughter actually wore to the prom. She debated just putting a coat on over the bathrobe she'd been living in, but decided that was a little too depressed-looking, even for her current mood. In shapeless wool pants that were well past their prime and, yes, the beige sweater again, she set out in her car.

The lights were on in the Town Hall. The janitor must be there waiting for her. She got out her key, but the front door was open. "Everett," she called out, but nobody answered.

She scanned the large, lofty room, and her breath caught in her throat. At the back was an easel holding a painting. Slowly she stepped forward. As she approached, she recognized Ian's unique style, but something was different. The colors were subdued, and it wasn't a landscape. She moved a little faster.

The painting showed, unmistakably, her behind a podium in a professional-looking beige suit, an impressionistic American flag forming the background of the scene. That was Nick sitting on the podium, his flaming red hair matching hers, and behind them, one arm around her and Nick and the other holding a dark-haired infant, was Ian.

It was a painting of her dream fulfilled, and her family a solid unit behind her.

Tansy could barely breathe as she peered at the plaque at the bottom of the handsome walnut frame. The painting was titled *The Proposal*.

She quivered inside, and her eyes stung with tears on the brink of falling. She heard footsteps and whirled to see Ian coming slowly down the length of the room to stand beside her. His face was expressionless, but his eyes told her everything she needed to know.

"A simple yes or no will do," he said softly.

She gazed at him, her heart welling up with love. She shook her head. "I'm sorry," she said.

His face hardened. He was struggling to hold back his disappointment, his sadness. She couldn't let him suffer long.

"I simply can't. Not until you paint my jacket orange."

Ian's face lit up with a smile, and then a miracle happened. He began to laugh, a strong, happy laugh, a belly laugh. Maybe he hadn't ever laughed—until now. Flinging her arms around him, Tansy held him tight, the laughter vibrating in her hair as he crushed her to his chest.

"Oh, Tansy," he murmured, his voice choked, "I love you so much, you little devil."

"Not as much as I love you."

They clung together, comforting each other for the agony they'd endured.

At last Ian whispered in her ear, "You still haven't answered my question."

"Oh," she breathed. "I thought I had." She drew back and gave him a wicked smile. "A few strokes of orange paint and my answer is yes."

"Yes," Ian shouted, making the rafters of the old hall shake and deafening Tansy. "Can everybody in town hear me? She said yes!"

Epilogue

New Year's Eve...

Lilah and Allie had insisted on a party, and those wimps, Daniel and Mike, had backed them up.

Not even Tansy had stood by him. Instead, she'd clapped her pretty little hands and said, "We'll make it a New Year's Eve party! Invite everybody! Have it in Town Hall!"

Okay, a party to announce their engagement was one thing, but in Town Hall?

The answer to that was yes, and here Ian stood, like a fish out of water. He was surrounded by everybody in Serenity Valley except the ones who were sick, or in the last stages of labor, or taking care of the sick, or standing over the mother-to-be, ready to deliver the baby.

And he'd never felt happier.

He'd be having a show in New York in April, and if that Bunny person even thought about making him come to the opening, he'd—

Well, he'd probably go to the opening. In a tuxedo.

Since he was about to become an *artiste,* a social butterfly, man about town and possibly Tansy's First

Gentleman one day, he'd give himself the pleasure, one last time, of standing back and observing instead of joining in.

Tansy was the center of a group, all chattering happily. She was vibrant in a bright green dress, and Ian paused to let his eyes wander over her small body, her slender curves. On Valentine's Day she'd be his to have and to hold forever.

Nick stood with her, and she held his hand while he gazed up at her as if she were an angel. *Ha,* Ian thought fondly. *She's no angel.*

Daniel was sticking so close to Lilah they moved as one person. Lilah glowed with happiness and good health, while Daniel was already behaving in that concerned way expectant fathers did.

Daniel's foster boys were all there, plus his adopted sons. They were chortling together in a corner, obviously enjoying each other's company.

Allie was flitting around the room, her dark hair swinging over the shoulders of her stylish black dress, probably still talking about her and Mike's Christmas Eve wedding, which, he had to admit, had been pretty spectacular. The reception had lasted so late that he remembered Christmas Day only hazily.

Allie would start taking courses in mid-January, working on her Ph.D. in clinical psychology. Smart lady, especially smart to have fallen in love with Mike.

Mike, holding on his left hip the half brother his father had left him in his will, of all things, followed behind her. They'd leave for their honeymoon in a few days, "When business at the diner is slow and Allie's classes haven't started yet," Mike had explained. But from the look on his face, Ian suspected the honeymoon had already begun and would last a long, long time.

Ian's gaze drifted farther. His farmhands, Edna, Joe and Tim, were all there, and all dressed up. The Appletrees huddled with Allie's parents, probably consulting Allie on important matters like wedding dresses, flower arrangements and how they could talk Tansy down from an orange-and-cream color scheme to, at least, soft coral and cream.

The older guests were gathered around tables, eating the array of hors d'oeuvres Mike had catered and looking as if they could make it to midnight as easily as any of "those young folks" could. A group of middle-aged women stood together, nodding their heads and looking serious, either talking about the state of the world or whether Hilda or Peggy made the best peppermint brownies, and why they were both so selfish with the recipe.

One day, he hoped, his mother would join that group, that she'd be clean and sober and stay that way for the rest of her life. And that the valley would accept her, just as they'd accepted the truth the Foster brothers had kept hidden for so many years. Good people. Good place to live.

They'd come so far, he and Daniel and Mike, from misery and anger to happiness beyond anything they could imagine. Ian felt such strong emotions rising inside him that he knew he had to be with Tansy.

Yes, he was actually tired of standing back, being an observer. He was ready to be in the middle of the fray. That, too, was something he couldn't have imagined.

Tansy was gazing at him, and he swiftly crossed the floor. "Time for the announcement?" he asked.

Her eyes twinkled and her mouth twitched. "You've been dreading it so much, and now you're suggesting it's time?"

"Yep," Ian said. "I've changed."

Her smile faded, replaced by an expression so full of love that he had to struggle with his emotions again. "Don't change too much," she said softly. "I adore you just as you are." The smile came back. "The way you are now, anyway. In love with me."

He led her to the back of the room, where the boys had set up a tiny stage, and ushered her up the single step. Mike clanged a fork against a champagne glass and the hubbub faded.

"Thank you for being here tonight," Ian said, "to celebrate the New Year with the Foster family." He waited for the clapping to subside, then put his arm around Tansy, who snuggled into him.

"But we have something else to celebrate," he went on. "My engagement to Mayor Tansy Appletree—"

"*And* mine to Ian Foster," Tansy chimed in, flashing her ring and hugging him even tighter.

There was a ripple of laughter, and though the announcement didn't come as a surprise to any of the guests, the clapping was accompanied by cheers and raised champagne glasses.

Ian could tell he was about to do something he'd never done before. He didn't know if he should, but darn it, he was going to anyway. "And now, milady," he said loudly enough for the whole room to hear, "shall we dance?"

Tansy's startled expression as he swept her off the

stage and onto the floor was worth the embarrassment. Music, stopped for the announcement, started up again, an uncertain rendition of "Shall We Dance?" as Tansy whispered into his throat, "Oh, yes, I want to dance with you forever."

And locked into each other's arms, they sailed through the room, through the people who loved them, toward their future together.

Kay Young returned to woozy consciousness to find
that she was lying on a soft sofa beneath a heap of quilts
near a cheerfully burning fire. When she tried to move,
however, everything hurt, and she groaned.

At once she heard a sound, then a stranger with a
hard, harsh face was squatting beside her. "Shh," he
said softly. "You're safe here. I promise."

"I have to go," she said weakly, struggling against
pain. "He'll find me. He can't find me."

"Easy, lady," he said quietly. "You're hurt. No one's
going to find you here."

"He will," she said desperately, terror clutching at
her insides. "He always finds me!"

"Easy," he said again. "There's a blizzard outside. No
one's getting here tonight, not even the doctor. I know,
because I tried."

"Doctor? I don't need a doctor! I've got to get
away."

"There's nowhere to go tonight," he said levelly. "And
if I thought you could stand, I'd take you to a window
and show you."

But even as she tried once more to pull away the
quilts, she remembered something else: this man had

been gentle when he'd found her beside the road, even when she had kicked and clawed. He hadn't hurt her.

Terror receded just a bit. She looked at him and detected signs of true concern there.

The terror eased another notch and she let her head sag on the pillow. "He always finds me," she whispered.

"Not here. Not tonight. That much I can guarantee."

Will Kay's mysterious rescuer protect
her from her worst fears?
Find out in HER HERO IN HIDING by
New York Times *bestselling author Rachel Lee.*
Available June 2010, only from
Silhouette® Romantic Suspense.

HARLEQUIN® Romance®

GIRLS' Weekend in VEGAS

Four friends, four dream weddings!

On a girly weekend in Las Vegas, best friends Alex, Molly, Serena and Jayne are supposed to just have fun and forget men, but they end up meeting their perfect matches! Will the love they find in Vegas stay in Vegas?

Find out in this sassy, fun and wildly romantic miniseries all about love and friendship!

Saving Cinderella! by MYRNA MACKENZIE
Available June

Vegas Pregnancy Surprise by SHIRLEY JUMP
Available July

Inconveniently Wed! by JACKIE BRAUN
Available August

Wedding Date with the Best Man
by MELISSA McCLONE
Available September

www.eHarlequin.com

HRI7663

Silhouette *Desire*

From *USA TODAY* bestselling author

LEANNE BANKS

CEO'S EXPECTANT SECRETARY

Elle Linton is hiding more than just her affair with her boss Brock Maddox. And she's terrifed that if their secret turns public her mother's life may be put at risk. When she unexpectedly becomes pregnant she's forced to make a decision. Will she be able to save her relationship and her mother's life?

Available June
wherever books are sold.

Always Powerful, Passionate and Provocative.

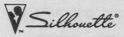

ROMANTIC SUSPENSE

Sparked by Danger, Fueled by Passion.

NEW YORK TIMES AND USA TODAY
BESTSELLING AUTHOR

RACHEL LEE

BRINGS YOU AN ALL-NEW
CONARD COUNTY: THE NEXT GENERATION SAGA!

After finding the injured Kay Young on a deserted country
road Clint Ardmore learns that she is not only being hunted
by a serial killer, but is also three months pregnant.
He is determined to protect them—even if it means
forgoing the solitude that he has come to appreciate.
But will Clint grow fond of having an attractive woman
occupy his otherwise empty ranch?

Find out in

Her Hero in Hiding

Available June 2010 wherever books are sold.

Visit Silhouette Books at www.eHarlequin.com

SRS27681

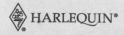

HARLEQUIN®

Showcase

Vicki Lewis Thompson

On sale May 11, 2010

Reader favorites from the most talented voices in romance

Save $1.00 on the purchase of 1 or more Harlequin® Showcase books.

SAVE $1.00

on the purchase of 1 or more Harlequin® Showcase books.

Coupon expires Oct 31, 2010. Redeemable at participating retail outlets. Limit one coupon per purchase. Valid in the U.S.A. and Canada only.

52609015

Canadian Retailers: Harlequin Enterprises Limited will pay the face value of this coupon plus 10.25¢ if submitted by customer for this product only. Any other use constitutes fraud. Coupon is nonassignable. Void if taxed, prohibited or restricted by law. Consumer must pay any government taxes. Void if copied. Nielsen Clearing House ("NCH") customers submit coupons and proof of sales to Harlequin Enterprises Limited, P.O. Box 3000, Saint John, NB E2L 4L3, Canada. Non-NCH retailer—for reimbursement submit coupons and proof of sales directly to Harlequin Enterprises Limited, Retail Marketing Department, 225 Duncan Mill Rd., Don Mills, ON M3B 3K9, Canada.

5 65373 00076 2 (8100)0 11651

U.S. Retailers: Harlequin Enterprises Limited will pay the face value of this coupon plus 8¢ if submitted by customer for this product only. Any other use constitutes fraud. Coupon is nonassignable. Void if taxed, prohibited or restricted by law. Consumer must pay any government taxes. Void if copied. For reimbursement submit coupons and proof of sales directly to Harlequin Enterprises Limited, P.O. Box 880478, El Paso, TX 88588-0478, U.S.A. Cash value 1/100 cents.

HARLEQUIN®

COMING NEXT MONTH

Available June 8, 2010

#1309 THE SHERIFF AND THE BABY
Babies & Bachelors USA
C.C. Coburn

#1310 WALKER: THE RODEO LEGEND
The Codys: The First Family of Rodeo
Rebecca Winters

#1311 THE BEST MAN IN TEXAS
Tanya Michaels

#1312 SECOND CHANCE HERO
Shelley Galloway

www.eHarlequin.com